MISTRESS ANGEL

London, 1357. Once a child bride, married off to halt a blood feud between rich and ambitious families, Isabella is now a tormented young widow. When her beloved son Matthew is torn away from her care, spirited somewhere into the country by her malicious in-laws, Isabella is desperate. To save her son she will do anything, risk anything. Even if it means she must lose the love of her life, the handsome armorer Stephen Fletcher . . .

LINDSAY TOWNSEND

MISTRESS ANGEL

Complete and Unabridged

LINFORD
Leicester

First published in Great Britain in 2013

First Linford Edition
published 2014

A catalogue record for this book is available
from the British Library.

ISBN 978–1–4448–2157–4

Published by
F. A. Thorpe (Publishing)
Anstey, Leicestershire

Set by Words & Graphics Ltd.
Anstey, Leicestershire
Printed and bound in Great Britain by
T. J. International Ltd., Padstow, Cornwall

This book is printed on acid-free paper

1

London, May 1357

Isabella was reading a scolding letter from her mother when Sir William's man-servant John stepped into the workshop and jerked his head to the outside, holding the door open for her.

She tucked the scrap of parchment into her belt and hurried into the back yard, lifting her skirts clear of the cloying mud. It was raining still, a light spring drizzle that had lasted for days and stirred up the usual offal and dung stink of London. She wrinkled her nose and covered her mouth with her hand.

'Hurry!' John urged. 'The master does not like to be kept waiting.'

Isabella picked her way round a deep cart track and made for the stand of cherry and apple trees against the back boundary wall of her husband's family

1

house. The tall, portly figure waiting beneath these trees was unmistakable, as was his goldsmith's livery, worn by most guild members only on festivals and holy days but as a regular costume by him. She bowed her head.

Sir William waved his servant away. 'You are too brown,' he grumbled as Isabella approached. 'Are you a washer-wench, to be so brown? That will not do.'

Naturally I am tanned, through outdoor work. She had been instructed by her husband's family to weed the garden plot and gather greens daily, all work beneath her, but Isabella knew better than to protest. 'My son?' she asked quickly.

Sir William dismissed her anxious question with a sharp shake of his head. 'Later,' he snapped. 'When you prove your worth to us.'

Isabella fixed her eyes on the golden tips of Sir William's gilt-edged shoes and strove to appear calm. She had been hearing variations of this and other complaints for years, and they held no sting for her. The absence of her son was altogether different. *When may I see my child? It has been months since Richard took him from me and his family still keep us apart. Had I the means I would go to the law, for in this household no one listens to me. How does my son fare? Does Matthew think of me?* She longed to ask all of these things.

'How long have you been with us, Isabella?'

'For six years, since I wed your nephew.'

She had been married to Richard at twelve, made pregnant two years later and widowed three years after that, following a long and bitter apprenticeship of wedlock. *I have been a widow for six months and I do not miss a moment of my marriage.*

She sensed Sir William staring at her, stroking first his squirrel-fur cloak, then his neatly-trimmed beard. She resisted the impulse to shudder.

'You are much improved in looks of late,' he remarked.

Yes, not being beaten nightly by a drunken brute improves a woman's appearance. Isabella raised her head. 'May I see Matthew?'

Sir William frowned at the second mention of her son. 'Did I not say later? Have you a better gown?'

Accustomed to his abrupt manner, Isabella said nothing. Sir William need only check the household accounts to realize she had three dresses. One was her bridal gown, a tiny, wrinkled dress, worn with such hopes when she was still only a child. She could scarcely bear to look at it now.

'We must have you robed in brighter colors,' Sir William continued. 'And you must stay indoors. Wash your face in whatever women use to whiten skin. You must shine like a jewel.'

When she was first married, Isabella had been full of questions, until Richard's ready fists had silenced her. She nodded to show she understood

4

and waited to be told more. *Perhaps I am to be married again*, she thought, and hoped this time the man would be kind. *Please let him bring my son Matthew back from wherever he is living and safe into our home. If my new husband does that, I will love him forever.*

Sir William picked a spray of cherry blossom and held it alongside her face. 'Yes, you shall do very well,' he rumbled. 'Your dowry is gone, you failed in your marriage task, you have no great skills, but we can put that beauty of yours to work.'

Abruptly, he seized the front of her bodice and yanked on the loose cloth, half-exposing her breasts. Isabella covered herself with an arm but did not resist or utter a sound. If feigning acquiescence brought her news of her son she would be as still and silent as a grave.

'Good, good.' Sir William strolled around her, pinching her flanks, muttering, 'She needs a touch more flesh here, but her breasts are still ripe, for all her nursing of that pup.'

Surely he would tell me if Matthew is dead? She had not set eyes on her son for seven months, since Richard had spitefully sent him off to another household, somewhere in Kent. *My husband did that just before he was killed, murdered in a blood-feud not of my making but for which I am still blamed. When will it end?*

'You will oblige me,' Sir William went on, and he took her roughly by her shoulder and half-turned her, back to the house. 'There, look at your son now. Not one word.'

Isabella blinked the drizzle from her eyes and stared at the small, thin figure standing with his back to her in the open doorway to the workshop.

It was Matthew, clothed in the belted blue cloak and cap she had made for him last winter, his fair, curling hair a little longer and more sun-bleached than when she had last seen him. He was growing and carried himself very straight, she thought proudly. She took a step forward, closer to him. *He was no more than a baby when Richard ripped him from me. Now he is a little boy of four years old, just four.*

'No nearer,' warned Sir William. 'That is enough.'

He gestured to someone at the house and the door closed, cutting Isabella off from that too-brief glimpse. Heart-scalded, she swung round. 'Please, let me speak to Matthew,' she begged. *Let me hold him, embrace him, smell him, hug him.* Relief that he was alive washed through her, making her weak when she had to be strong.

'To business,' Sir William remarked dryly, watching her fumbling with her gown strings, his eyes bright, with the pitiless interest of a bird. 'You have seen the boy, now heed my terms.'

Isabella chewed on the inside of her cheek to stop a rising cry, glad that the rain hid her tears. She nodded in silence, bracing herself.

Even now, Matthew must not know I

am here. Surely if he did he would come to me? And will I see him again? How long will he stay?

Sir William smiled. 'You will do much, make great efforts to see your son again?' He did not wait for an answer. 'This family needs to make good alliances, and you are available. Stephen Fletcher I thought. He is armourer to Duke Henry himself, and widowed.'

His smile widened and his hard dark eyes sparkled with open malice. 'I understand he is like you, the offspring of a commoner. Some would call him a blacksmith. You should do well with him.'

Isabella felt her face flush with anger. 'And how, pray, will I meet him?'

'Use what wit you have, girl, and find out!' He pinched her cheek, hard, and moved away, tossing her final orders as he strolled off. 'I shall expect strong progress in your suit, Isabella. Win him within the month, become his mistress, extract rich gifts and favors from him, or you shall not see your son again. I will adopt Matthew as my own.'

He went inside, out of the rain, and slammed the door in her face.

⋆　⋆　⋆

Isabella ran after him, but Matthew was already gone. Her heart aching inside her chest and desperate to escape the ready complaints of her mother-in-law, she claimed that Sir William asked her to collect a parcel of herbs from the apothecary. Outside again in the rain, she stumbled by way of the back lanes to the house and shop of her friend, Amice the Spicer.

Amice took one look at her and drew Isabella behind the curtain at the back of her shop, where she had a bed she slept in when guarding a fresh batch of cinnamon from burglars.

'Get under the covers and warm up,' she said, in her brisk, managing way. 'As you see, the shop is quiet now, so we can talk. Have you received another letter from that prating mother of yours, blaming you for a feud not of your making? I presume your own flesh-and-blood have not welcomed you back?'

'No, they have not.' Isabella shook as she stumbled into the bed. *I do not think they will ever do so*. Like Amice she knew that, according to custom, she might have returned to her own family, now that Richard was dead. Her parents, however, had cast her off. Her mother still wrote letters, but only to instruct her and to complain. *To my parents I am one of the Martintons now*. It was a terrifying thought, one she dared not dwell on.

'Is your mother-in-law expecting you to spin gold from straw or some other foolishness?'

Amice's ironic question returned her to the present. *A present even harder than my past*. 'I saw Matthew,' Isabella burst out through chattering lips. 'They would not let me speak to him. He did not even know I was behind him.'

'Ah, that old cruelty.'

The sympathy in Amice's warm voice brought Isabella to tears. She shuddered violently as her friend swept the warm, coarse blankets up to her ears.

'Rest first, then tell me everything.' Amice bustled out into the shop again, closed the shutters and returned to light a brazier. 'What did you say to get out of that wretched den?'

'That my uncle needs herbs.'

'I have those. I shall give you a bundle when you leave.'

Isabella closed her eyes for a moment, willing herself not to cry. Away from her reluctant family-by-wedlock and the thunderstorm tension of the household, she felt her constant headache begin to clear. It was marvelous, too, to be safe at Amice's, snug and warm in a low-gabled shop perfumed with spices. She sighed, sitting up with a pillow behind her head as her friend brought her a cup of warmed wine. 'Thank you.'

'None needed.' Amice batted aside

her gratitude. 'We both know what you did for me. It is my pleasure to help you in return, in any way I can.'

Isabella knew she meant it. They shared the cup between them, Amice telling of a Flemish merchant in the shop that morning, seeking pepper and saffron. Her black, strong-featured, full-lipped face was animated as she mimicked the accent of the Fleming, kicking her long legs against the wall as she reached the climax of her tale.

'Paid me a good fistful of gold and unclipped coins for a few threads of saffron and one of my kisses. The man seemed to think I was an Ethiope out of Egypt and said my mouth was a lucky charm. I kissed him once, on the cheek, and did not tell him I come from the back end of Cheapside.'

She chortled, finished the wine and put her dark, handsome head to one side. 'You smell calm again,' she announced. Amice was a believer in the scent of things. 'Will you have more wine? I have peppermint to disguise your breath from your mother-in-law.'

Isabella smiled and shook her head. Reaching inside her gown, beneath the drawstrings Sir William had so roughly parted, she found the three gold rings strung on a cord and handed the rings and ribbon to Amice.

'Sell or pawn?' Amice asked.

'Sell,' Isabella said firmly. These rings were the last of her dowry, hidden away by her and forgotten by Sir William, Richard's mother and her parents. 'I need a good price.'

Swiftly she explained why. 'I have only weeks to secure this Stephen Fletcher, and through him my son,' she concluded.

'A harsh undertaking,' Alice remarked. 'They are unkind people, your husband's kin.'

Isabella could not disagree but, thinking of the seemingly impossible task, she began to feel a coil of hope. 'The goldsmiths' guild is planning a great spectacle when Prince Edward brings the French king back with him to London. I need to bribe my way into it.'

'A good place to see and be seen, for sure. And Sir William swore you would have new gowns for this?' Amice held a ring set with a huge square sapphire close to the twisting flames of the brazier and gave a small grunt of satisfaction. 'This is fine.'

'Sir William promises many things, but I find they do not happen.'

Amice's keen eyes glittered. 'Then you are blamed.'

Isabella shrugged. 'I cannot afford to wait to see if he grants me fresh gowns. I have my son to consider.' *Matthew! How I wish I could have talked to you today, held you, kept you by me.*

'I will go today, before curfew.' Amice rattled the rings in her palm. 'Is any of this work Richard's? Let me avoid questions, if I can.'

'Have no fear on that score. I have and hold nothing of his.' *Which is why his kindred keep Matthew, as the only hold they have over me.*

She flinched as Amice brushed her wrist. 'I will bring the money tomorrow,' her friend said.

'Thank you,' Isabella murmured, wishing she could stay where she was until Amice returned. Knowing she must leave before she was missed in the workshop, she flung back the covers and scrambled to her feet. 'I do not know where I will be tomorrow. Sometimes my mother-in-law keeps me at home.'

'I will find you.'

★　★　★

The following day it was raining harder and foggy, a thick gray miasma coating the city roofs and towers. Isabella fretted about Amice having to visit her in this dismal murk, but her mother-in-law found an excuse to dispatch her into it.

'I have a fancy for oysters and malmsey,' Margery instructed, counting a few pennies into Isabella's hand. 'You

15

must go, girl, I can spare no other. Take the spit-boy with you as guide, though you do not really need one, do you? Not with your parents living so close by the docks.'

'Honored mother.' Knowing Margery would be irritated by that form of address, Isabella followed it up with a bow and stalked out into the pouring rain. She and the spit-boy scowled at each other until the end of the street, marched around a corner, shook hands and parted ways. Nigel was her ally, although both knew he was meant to spy on her for the family. Now they were free for an hour or so, and Isabella intended to make full use of the time.

She called on Amice first, but her friend was also out and Amice's limping apprentice had no idea where she could be found. Resigned to seeing Amice as God willed it, Isabella drew her molting fur cloak tightly about her shoulders and trod nimbly beneath the dripping jetties.

She loved being out in the city, part

of its vivid heart. She was always excited to be in London, even in the dreadful year of pestilence when Richard had taken Matthew and, with his kin, fled the city for their holding in East Ham. She and the prentices had been left in the workshop and it had been hard. When she did not dread the boils and bloody coughing she feared fire, or looters, but they had all come through — London had not failed her, even then. Now, slipping and sliding through the muddy alleys, avoiding shadowed corners, flicking a small coin to a beggar camped beneath a jetty, she heard a hundred different voices in the fog and a dozen different tongues and knew she was home.

Matthew should be with me, learning these streets.

She did not make for the docks. Oyster and wine sellers thronged the city, so she wasted no effort on the wharves where wine barrels were unloaded. She had no desire to encounter her father, although he had lately grown so rich as a vintner that he might not trouble to be out on such a day.

Reflected in the pallid fog, a moving, closing shadow shimmered against the wattle wall of the house opposite. Frustrated by her small, female state, Isabella hunched into a doorway and waited until the creeping footpad vanished along another narrow lane. Amice stalked these alleys like a warrior but Amice was tall and knew how to fight with a knife. Shorter by half a head and allowed no decent blades, Isabella was constantly reminded of how easily she could be mauled. Had Richard not proved that, night after night?

Hearing the bells of great Saint Paul's thundering above her, watching the hop-and-skip of folk darting in and out of the rain, she waited until she could make out the raucous calls of the street sellers again. Moving on, she turned off the house-step — straight into the path of a man leading a bay horse and eating a pie.

'Hold there!'

The stranger tossed his pie to a shivering urchin and caught Isabella as she slithered back, his grip firm but not cruel. 'If you would be a cut-purse, girl, you need to be quieter.' He stared down at her while his horse chewed on a slither of hanging roof-thatch and a water-seller shouldered past them both, muttering curses.

'Forgive me, sir.' Isabella did not recognize the man but she was keen to be on her way. He was taller than Amice and almost as dark, with a tanned, clean-shaven face and penetrating eyes. Green-gray eyes, she realized with a jolt, as he plucked her off the step and up onto the saddle of his mount with the same ease as she might lift a toddler.

'Unhand me!'

'Where are you going?' he asked, ignoring her protest. She began to slide off the back of the glossy bay but he anticipated that move and stopped her simply by catching her foot.

'Sir!'

'This is neither the weather nor the place for a decent maid,' he went on, his green-gray eyes sparkling with amusement as she glowered at him. 'Let me take you where you need to be.'

Isabella knew she looked like a servant. 'Why would you do that?'

He grinned and released her foot. 'Even beggars deserve kindness now and then. Besides, you did not get those good teeth and fine accents on any midden heap. Now, where should I carry you away to?'

They were moving, Isabella realized, the horse piling through a vast puddle with the man splashing carelessly alongside. Another moment and they would be within sight of the grand houses and palaces of the river, and, to the north, the goldsmiths' new guildhall, still being built.

It would not do for him to escort her there with so many wagging tongues eager to take the news to Sir William. *If need be, I shall tell my own gossip and, please God, be rewarded for it with a visit to or from my son.*

'Here,' she called, pointing to a small glover's shop tucked around the corner of a crooked alley. 'This is my place.'

The stranger reined in at once. Before Isabella could stir he swept her off his horse and lightly onto the cobbles, nodding to the wide-eyed glover. 'I will see you safe within.'

'There is no need.' Conscious of his height and breadth and easy strength, Isabella felt heat tiding into her face. She prayed she was not blushing. 'Thank you for your help, Sir . . . ?'

He smiled, his eyes still bright with amusement, and answered readily, 'Stephen Fletcher, at your service, Mistress Angel.'

Isabella automatically gasped. *The very man I have to win!* All calculation deserted her as they stared at each other. *What will it be like to be in Stephen's arms? What will his kisses be like?*

Heedless of the prickling rain, Stephen studied her for a long moment, his eyes narrowing as if he guessed her thoughts.

Isabella forced herself to bow her head, her breath threatening to stop as she waited, crucified by his silence. *What now? Should I say more, do more?*

She felt a gentle touch, softer than rain, brush against her cheek.

'I pass this way tomorrow,' he said softly. 'I need new gloves.'

'I shall be here.' *Why did I say that? 'Tis madness to promise anything!*

'Until tomorrow, Mistress Angel.' Stroking another raindrop from her flushed face and raising a hand in farewell, Stephen mounted his bay and cantered off in the direction of the river.

2

Within the great hall of her dead husband's kindred, Isabella stood, as ordered, beside the small spring fire and traced a fire tong with her foot. She had sent a messenger to Sir William, informing him of her chance encounter with Stephen Fletcher, and hoped her uncle would allow her to see Matthew in return. That hope had been swiftly dashed.

Sir William leaned forward on his seat. 'You did not tell Stephen Fletcher your name?'

'There was no time. But I will return to the glovers to wait for him and then — '

'Absolutely not!' Sir William leapt to his feet. 'He must see you as a lady to be wooed and won, not a common strumpet!'

'You said I should be available and

willing to be his mistress.'

Sir William stormed from the dais and slapped her. 'Do not be insolent with me! You present yourself as a gentlewoman. Stephen Fletcher is the armorer to the duke, not a stable-hand!'

'Not a blacksmith then?' Isabella countered, amazed at herself. 'I have a plan for that,' she went on, with a steely calmness she did not feel. 'Sir Nicholas has approved it.'

At the mention of one of the most powerful men in the goldsmiths' guild, Sir William became very still and quiet. 'How is this possible?' he demanded. 'How do you even know him?'

'I agreed the details yesterday, while I was out fetching wine and oysters,' Isabella replied. 'I am one of the maidens in the golden cages.'

That silenced her uncle by marriage, but it gave her little satisfaction. *Still Sir William will not let me visit my son.*

Her face smarted and her teeth ached but that was nothing. The tears blurring her vision were not because of the slap.

I hoped, really hoped, that he would let me see Matthew again. Sometimes she feared that he would never relent.

★　★　★

A few days later, Isabella, with a frowning Amice hovering close, climbed carefully out of the jetty window of Sir Nicholas' house and into a tall, gilded cage suspended above the cobbles of Cheapside. The dawning May sun glittered on the fragile walls of her 'prison' and the road below was unusually clean. She had been one of those sent out to scrub the cobbles only the day before.

'Fine weather at last and a good day for the procession,' Amice remarked, her hands gripped firmly on the window ledge. 'But it will be hours yet.'

Isabella shrugged. 'I am here now.' *And out of reach of my kindred, should they change their minds and decide another of the family's womenfolk should bring honor to this spot.*

Amice tugged on the cage, her dark brows heavy with suspicion. 'The front of this is very low. Mind you do not take a fainting fit and tumble out.'

Isabella smiled and reached back through the window to hug her friend. 'I shall be very well. Have you the gold and silver flowers?'

'Safe in a basket at my feet. Listen! The church bells are chiming. It will soon begin.'

Isabella felt a frisson of excitement though, as Amice had said, it would be hours yet before the procession reached her cage. It would take an age for all the grand folk to cross the city, the members of the guilds, all in their livery, Prince Edward and his retinue, and finally the captured French king. Her Londoners were a curious people and they would gather in their hundreds to witness this fine spectacle. Already she could see crowds clustering in the nearby streets and men and women in the houses looking down onto Cheapside, opening the shutters of their upper windows to enjoy the view. She leaned out and looked toward the looming spire of Saint Paul's, along the broad, smooth road known simply as *The Street* in the city, where the goldsmiths had their shops and houses.

'Be careful, Issa,' Amice whispered urgently behind her. 'You are no use to Matthew with a broken neck.'

But it is so glorious today, so warm and gold. The sky is like a cornflower. I know all will be well. It must be well. Isabella turned and smiled to reassure her friend. Stretching out her hands, she clasped Amice's, tight about the window ledge. 'Why not go downstairs?' she said softly, aware of her friend's dislike of heights. 'You will be closer to the princes, when they come.'

Amice shook her head, her dark curls flying. 'Closer to lewd fellows and sweaty prentices, too.'

'For today the street is filled with rose petals,' Isabella tempted her.

'For today I shall stay here, as I promised, with you.' Amice swallowed and deliberately unclenched her fists, planting her hands on her hips and her head on one side. 'You are saffron-bright today, Issa, and you smell better.'

'Thanks to your perfumes,' Isabella laughed, flicking one of the long gold earrings that Amice habitually wore and silently admiring her companion's elegant, red velvet gown. Her own dress was more ornate, a pink tunic over a green kirtle with trailing sleeves, richly embroidered in gold with the badges of Sir William's family. She wore a gold crespine in her red-gold hair and her mother-in-law Margery had insisted she don a pair of white gloves that already felt sticky. 'Do you think the French king will be handsome?'

'We shall see. I am more interested to see your man. You will point him out to me?'

'Of course.' Horns blew in the distance and Isabella turned to face *The Street* again, wondering how long it would be before she caught sight of Stephen in the retinue of the duke.

'It is good that you know what he looks like, though no thanks to your family.'

'I think he will be kind,' Isabella murmured, to reassure herself.

Behind her, Amice made a sound in her throat to show that she was less than convinced. 'What will he do if he sees you? If he recognizes you and thinks you duped him in your first meeting?'

'He is kind,' Isabella repeated. 'I am sure of it.' *Soon I will know and pray God I am right.*

For now she could only wait and watch and pick her time to fall, as fall she must.

★ ★ ★

His daughter slept in his arms now, so peacefully. Stephen did not want to leave her. He did not want to venture back into the slop bucket of London and parade like a dancing bear with the nobles and great of the city. His daughter was finally at rest and he wanted to stay with her.

Stephen frowned and rolled his powerful shoulders, spying the pink and gold of dawn through the small gap in the closed shutter casement and regarding it not as the blessing of a new day but an ever-present challenge. These breathing fits of Joanna's terrified her and racked him with impotent despair. Before his wife Cecilia had died his daughter had been a bright, spirited girl and had never sickened. He had striven for honor and power, proud of his skill, eager to show off his connections to Duke Henry, the foremost knight of the world. He had married Cecilia for her wit, bearing and land and had never expected to love her. Unlacing, happy love had ambushed him all the same. She had become his moon and sun, cool, tranquil and elegant by day, rosy, glowing and tingling by night.

His wife haunted him. He sought her in dreams and in the outer world — a warm glance from a woman, the call or gesture of some unknown girl were all sweet reminders of Cecilia, who lived anew in them for him.

'How can she be dead?' he muttered, twitching away at the thought as a horse does at a gadfly. Joanna, sucking her thumb, rolled in his arms as Cecilia had once rolled in bed toward him and he grieved afresh. 'How could she leave us?'

It had not been the pestilence, but she had been three days in the dying, trying to expel his son in a long, dreadful child-birth. The midwife had urged him to save the boy but he had wanted Cecilia, not some changeling stranger. In the bitter end he had lost them both and the world had turned gray, the charge after glory meaningless. He was two years a widower and still his grief was battle-sword sharp at times.

The door to the small solar at the back of the timber house creaked open and his sister bustled in. 'Still not groomed, Stevie?' she scolded, lifting

Joanna from his arms and tucking the child into the small bed beneath the window. 'You should look your best and who knows? You may see your London glover's girl again.'

Stephen grunted a response, wishing he had never spoken of the lass. Worse, Bedelia knew he had returned to the city to watch for her — his sister never said anything but he knew she knew.

'tis all folly, he told himself, for the wench had vanished, as teasing and unreal as the glass nail he had once been told to find when first apprenticed. She had been a spirited creature, too, with a sadness clinging about her slender limbs as if she had lost someone dear. He would have liked to discover more of her, but then it was plain her life was not her own. He had searched several glovers' shops for her, without success.

'Probably married,' he remarked, sensing his older sister's knowing glance on him. 'Certainly a liar. All women are.' He rose and stretched, putting his palms on the white-washed ceiling.

'Nonsense. I have lit a candle in church for you to find her again.'

Stephen shot a quick look at Joanna in case she overheard and thought him disrespectful to her mother, but his daughter slumbered on, coiled in the sheets like a baby hedgehog in leaves. 'You will let her sleep?'

'Until she wakes by nature.'

'You meddle, sister.'

'Nonsense!' Bedelia flicked him with her spindle as he edged past her. She was tall, as he was, and handsome, especially when her features were animated, as they were now. 'If our saint denies me a good wax candle on this bright day it is a poor thing. But you, set to! Shave your chin, comb your hair, wash your face.'

'Yes, mamma.' Bedelia's husband Alan was a merchant and Stephen lodged at their house when Alan was away at sea. *My sister forgets I am not a child anymore, though I bless her for her care of my Joanna.* He slipped round the door and strode off into the great hall to escape more instructions. The blaze of sunshine through the narrow minstrel's gallery put him in mind of the mystery girl's red-gold eyebrows and lashes and he grinned, finally catching the promise of the day.

London is a spit-pot but the girl is there somewhere and today, with the guilds scrambling to display for the French king, I will find her again, pray God. She had reminded him of Cecilia, but different, intriguing.

The quest pleased him and he broke into a run, hurrying to meet the day.

* * *

Two hours later, riding his most docile horse with his best hunting dog trotting alongside, Stephen resigned himself to the spectacle. His father would have loved all of this, his being in London, part of the retinue of Duke Henry and Prince Edward, close enough so he could actually see the French king's stately white palfrey and almost touch the captive monarch's rich black tunic. Cecilia would have loved the scattered rose petals, the gleaming streets and the kingfisher brightness of the English knights, arrayed in their best. He was less pleased to be in a stiff new tunic and tight new hose, the more so since one of the knights of the garter had hissed in his ear to be on the look out for lurking assassins on the roof-tops.

'The merchants promise the streets are safe but what do they know?' the burly knight had spat. 'Duke Henry wants you to look, you have the keenest eyes.' *And a wicked way with a throwing knife* the knight might have added, as both of them knew it.

So he was watching, guarding, and mighty glad of his lord's trust. But, as he twisted to and fro in the saddle, glancing from roof top to roof top, the new cloth chafed the back of his neck.

Going soft, Stephen? Ignoring the bawling of the mob he fixed on the jetties and roof tiles, staring into shadows and sun-flashes. The gaudy troop of soldiers and knights, already shifting at a slow canter, settled into a meandering amble as the road through Cheapside broadened between the grander houses belonging to the members of the goldsmith's guild.

'Ici, là!' cried Prince Edward, sweeping a bejeweled gloved arm toward the upper storeys. Beside him, on his taller horse, the French king looked up and softly applauded. Stephen scanned the ridge tiles of the freshly-painted, gilded houses and glanced where the prince was pointing.

There she is. He smiled.

He recognized her instantly by the proud tilt of her head, her sweetly handsome profile and those glowing eyes, more compelling even than the luxuriant gold of her hair or her sumptuous costume.

Goldsmith's garb and no glover's girl for sure, he thought, reining in his horse and slowing to admire her the more as she shimmered above him like the evening star. Encased in a narrow cage of gold suspended above the cobbles, he saw that she was one of twelve maidens positioned high above the street, all caged, all lovely, but his gaze returned to her alone. Already the others seemed pale shadows, water ripples, echoes. *But she is stunning.* Above the roar of blood in his ears he heard the ribald comments of Prince Edward and knew he also approved of her.

By a mighty effort of will Stephen tore his attention away from this bewitching, naughty beauty and returned to scanning roofscapes. Still his eyes kept flitting back as he silently willed her to turn within her cage, to look out, to look back, to see him.

Know me, girl. Wonder at me, as I do at you. He was torn between admiration and a longing to kiss her thoroughly for her deception. *Kissing you will be a sweet revenge.*

She was tossing flowers, delicate

metal posies of gold and silver that streaked the cobbles like flashing dew-drops or sun-flashed rain, pretty trinkets that the populace would certainly scramble for as soon as the nobles had passed. Still staring toward Westminster, although she must surely know by the mutter of the crowd that the foremost Prince of England and King of France rode right beneath her cage, she scattered another handful of golden petals, seemingly oblivious to the gasps of admiration. Silhouetted against the dark, smoke-stained jetty of the house, her slim body made a pleasing, subtle curve.

The picture she created then reminded him of Cecilia, dancing for him alone in their private chamber with her hair loose, spinning round on the spot with her dark locks flowing and her arms weaving around the bed-posts. Pierced by the memory he felt his horse stumble, crushing one of the metal flowers and rearing. He reined his mount in before it could trample any of the thronging crowd, speaking soothingly, gentling the beast and all the while watching the girl — the girl now, not Cecilia, not even in memory.

See me. Look at me.

★   ★   ★

Isabella's feet ached in her new shoes, her hands itched furiously within her new gloves and her face felt increasingly sun-scorched. Thinking of her son she kept smiling, throwing flowers, ignoring all Amice's mutterings at her back as the cage swung and tilted each time she stirred.

'The prince!' Amice called, her voice one of many as London cooed like doves, proud of its nobility today and even more of itself. Isabella knew the royal party was within feet of her, that soon the heir to the throne of England could reach up off his small black horse and brush the base of her cage with his gloved hand or feathered cap, but she held her pose of looking away. Somewhere, please all the saints, somewhere in that glittering retinue was surely Stephen Fletcher.

Please, Holy Mother, let him be here with his prince and lord, please, for the sake of my son.

She swung round in her cage, clasping one of the gilded wooden bars for support, giving Amice a quick smile to show she was safe and tipping another golden hailstorm of posies over the closing nobility. Pretending an imperiousness she was far from feeling, she lowered her head slowly, as if the retinues clustered in the street beneath her were as insignificant as bugs.

He's here! At once her breathing quickened as her body jolted. The gilded cage shook around her, as if caught in a sudden storm.

'He is here?' Forgetting her fear of heights, Amice leaned right out of the window. Isabella caught her back.

'Stephen is the tall, well-made man on the gray horse, just behind that fat knight of the garter,' she said, the admission huge in her mouth as if she was chewing on pebbles.

'Saffron and pepper, he is handsome! A man to dream of when he is not busy in your bed.'

'Amice!'

'Hush, Isabella, I speak my mind. Yes, your man is very fine, shapely and fine. Does he smell of mint? I wager he does. Not very colorful in his dress, though you can ginger him up, and my, his horse is old . . . '

Isabella did not hear the rest of her friend's pithy remarks. Looking down she was lost, her mind a whirlpool of thoughts and impressions as the rest of the street vanished to her. She had forgotten how magnetic his eyes were, with their soft tones of green and hard notes of gray, and how aquiline his nose. He was watching her, indulgence sparkling in his tanned, craggy face and tugging at the corners of his singer's mouth, as if he knew very well what she was about and did not care. Even in the earliest days of her marriage Richard had never stared at her like this, as if he

41

kissed her with his eyes.

He had caught one of her flowers, she realized as he held it aloft, showing it to her before tucking it away into one of his big, black, serviceable leather gloves.

'Fine as my best black pepper,' Amice was concluding, while Isabella struggled to hold onto herself, not abandon her sense utterly. *Remember Sir William's threats and the danger to Matthew.* She lifted her hand away from the edge of the cage and waved to the tall, strong figure below. *Stephen is surely my lord, my kind and noble lord, and I am forced to beguile him.* Shame engulfed her in a scalding tide.

I must do this, for Matthew.

Not in so extreme a way, her mind scolded, but it was as if her body no longer obeyed her reason. Stephen's smile was a welcome and in truth what time had she? In another moment he would be gone, passed, and her family would blame her. If she did not do this now they might never allow her to see her son.

It was the work of a single step and then done. As she forced her stiffened limbs to stir, Isabella glimpsed the rich tapestries, captured in France and hung from the first floors as trophies. She saw the shields, taken from the battlefield of Poitiers and ranged along the street in a triumphant display, glinting back at her. She thought of Matthew in his brave blue coat and fell out of the cage, a desperate launch, wondering if the cobbles would hurt. *Catch me, please catch me.*

In a slow fall, slow as a snail, she saw Stephen's smile falter, heard Amice's desperate, 'Issa!' and then she was floating, down and down.

Catch me, please catch me.

3

Stephen spurred his horse forward and snatched her from the air, stopping her headlong crash onto the street. His arms burned, sinews and tendons twisting and wrenching as he clung on, feeling her slip away. In that instant, when his shoulders felt dislocated and his groin rammed painfully against his saddle and his docile little gray nag whickered, close to a scream, he was near to yelling himself. How could one so slight and small weigh so much? Still she dragged him down to the ground, where the faint scatter of rose petals would give them no protection.

'Stay!' he roared, to himself, to her, as from the edge of his vision he saw the knight of the garter catch his horse's bridle, his bearded mouth a round 'O' of shock. Even Prince Edward, veteran of many a charge, had frozen.

He heard cloth ripping, wondered from the hot-metal sizzle in his arms if his muscles were ripping, and then it was over. She was netted in his grasp and whole.

I have caught a falling angel, he thought for a wild instant, and then the fancy was gone. He shook the stinging sweat from his eyes and looked at her, snug in his arms but gasping like a landed fish.

'Are you hurt?'

She shuddered, her eyes tightly shut like a child fearing punishment, her mouth trying to work as she fought to answer him. Any anger that he might have felt at her folly in leaning out so far vanished. He could tell — and he had seen enough battlefields to know — that she was uninjured in body, but shocked to her core. He saw, too, how very thin she was, and now, once fallen from her cage, how very pale.

'Peace, lass, you are safe.' He brought her before him onto his saddle, settling her sideways so she was cushioned against him. 'All is well.' He stroked her shivering limbs and heard the burly knight growl in his ear, 'You are excused duties, Fletcher, 'tis clearly safe enough. Take the silly wench away and let us move on.'

Around him, seeping back in tides of sound, he could hear the crowd gasping and applauding and Prince Edward saying to the French king that the maiden had been overcome by his royal presence.

Stephen dipped his head to the shivering girl. 'Forgive me, lady, I forgot myself in that moment. You are fallen a long way from a glovers' shop.'

Her eyes snapped open then, very blue and wide.

'Forgive me.' Her voice was low and sweet, but steady, as her breath was now steady. 'I am sorry, sir.'

'You should be, and I demand a forfeit.' Before he knew what he would do, Stephen was kissing her, gathering her even closer, her unguarded lips yielding and quivering under his. He ran his tongue across her teeth and caressed her mouth with his, sorry now to have startled her, but by God he had startled himself.

He broke their embrace, then, unable to stop himself, he kissed her again. Her skin was smooth as a pearl and inexorably he was drawn to the deep, enticing groove between her breasts . . .

Enough, man. Restraining himself, he lifted his head. 'No debt,' he said, stripping off a glove and cupping her flushed face with his hand.

'I am sorry,' she repeated, and then, more quietly, 'Thank you.'

'Move on!' grunted the knight, prodding his gray horse with his booted foot. 'You are holding up the prince!'

Abruptly, Stephen became aware again of the onlookers and nobility, the prince, Edward of Woodstock, smirking with a knowing expression on his long, narrow, bearded face and the retinue taking their cue from him, laughing as if he and the woman were court jesters. Keen to be away from their scrutiny,

Stephen reined back and turned his mount out of the procession into one of the side streets.

This alley was clogged with filth and rotting scraps, ankle deep in waste and rats. *I am mighty glad she did not fall down here.* Still, despite the sudden gloom and ordure stench he allowed his horse to plod at its own pace and his dog to browse and nose as it would, giving them all respite.

'My friend. Please, I must tell her I am safe,' his passenger whispered. 'She has such a dread of heights.'

'If she saw you fall, she knows I caught you.' Answering, Stephen remembered a tall black woman in a red dress, staring from an upper window. Recalling the black woman's horror, he felt aggrieved on her behalf and now sharpened his address to the girl. 'Were you overcome by the sight of the French king? I know he and Edward of Woodstock are both fair, and I have learned at court that such coloring is greatly admired.'

'I am not of the court,' she said at

once, then stopped. He knew then, from her tiny pause, that whatever she said next would be false. 'It is a very warm day, sir.'

'Indeed.' *And from that blush, you are a very poor liar.* Usually falsehood irked him but if there was more here than a simple misstep, he decided that he did not care. She had fallen out of her cage when he, Stephen, was passing. 'And now we meet again, Mistress Angel. Or should I say Mistress Truant?'

Her color deepened.

Enjoying himself, Stephen went on. 'You know my name, may I ask yours?'

'Isabella.' She cleared her throat. 'Isabella of London.'

'But no glover.'

It should have been impossible for her to blush any more but she did. 'I fear not.'

Had she trembled then? 'You have no need to fear. May I take you home, Isabella? That is, if you will admit to me where you live?'

She nodded once, then worried at her lower lip, her bright eyes as blue as cornflowers. No longer shaken, she still looked surprised, but then she could not be any more surprised than he himself. He had not done this kind of jesting for over two years, when he had gently teased Cecilia. For an instant he felt disloyal, yet where was the harm? 'Show me,' he coaxed.

★ ★ ★

Stephen was not smiling. Yet nor did he frown. He looked patient and quiet, his black eyebrows faintly raised as if he guessed and was amused by her confusion. 'Point my horse, then,' he said, while she was wondering what to say. When she nodded so he would not consider her entirely witless he grinned, his teeth a flash of white in his tanned face. She felt him urge his horse forward and the narrow shop fronts changed as they plodded on, passing a few stragglers in festive demon masks.

50

Be witty, amusing, available, threatened Sir William in her head, all traits that had been crushed in her by Richard. What would amuse a royal armourer, who mixed with princes and kings? *But he likes me.* She knew that from the way he held her, from his swift admiring glances whenever he thought she was looking elsewhere, and from his kiss. She wanted to bring her fingers to her mouth and trace where his sweet mouth had lingered.

I shall have much to reflect and dream on tonight, but I must not day-dream now.

Amice had been right, though. He tasted of mint and smelled of leather and a faint whiff of sulphur, perhaps from his time by the forges. What did he do as royal armourer? Did he ever use gold? That would be something in common between them. She opened her mouth to ask, then remembered just in time that he had not told her what he was or did, only his name. If she asked anything too close he might suspect her of seeking him out, of laying traps for him. *Which is exactly what I did and must do again.*

'Yes, my lady?' He must have sensed her question, possibly by her face. Richard had always mocked her for being too expressive.

They had reached the end of the alley and she pointed left. He turned the horse along another narrow lane, this one filled with stacked firewood and smelling of fish.

'Are you of London, Sir Stephen?' That was surely a safe inquiry.

'Not me, and no knight, either.' He admitted this without a seeming care, tucking his loose glove into his belt. He still wore the other, perhaps to keep the golden flower he had caught safe — she could only hope.

'I am of Kent,' he continued. 'I miss the orchards and fields there.'

'We have apple trees,' she began, stopping as it hit her afresh that Matthew was somewhere in Kent. *Surely the family will let me visit*

Matthew now? They must!

'Isabella of London,' Stephen went on, in a musing way. He leaned around a low-hanging jetty and tightened his grip about her waist as the horse ambled past a rooting pig. 'You like London? Of course you must, for you are of the goldsmiths and they live richly.'

'And you do not?' she replied, stung by his implied criticism. 'Your tunic is very fine, embroidered silk, I think, though you have burst a seam on the shoulder. I can mend it for you if you wish.'

What have I said? she thought desperately, as Stephen's piercing eyes narrowed and she braced herself for a set-down or worse, a blow. But even as she stiffened she realized he was laughing.

'A most generous offer, mistress! Should I remove it now?'

Her easy blush, which she so detested, roared up her face, stinging in her cheeks, but she was determined not

53

to be overcome. 'Not for me, sir. Your wife might not approve.'

Abruptly, like a candle being snuffed out, the light in his face vanished and he looked older, grimmer. 'I have none now — no wife, I mean. Where next?'

They had reached another junction of alleys. She pointed blindly right, cursing herself for her blunder in reminding Stephen of his dead wife and causing him grief, then realized too late that she had told him wrong. This way they were heading for the Vintry, the district of the wine merchants, a place of busy wharfs, warehouses and wine stalls, the place where her father did his business.

The thought of her father seeing her, spotting and ignoring her, as he always did whenever their paths crossed these days, made her shudder.

'Hey there. I would not have you faint again, or your kin will think me a ravisher.'

Stephen sounded truly concerned and she was ashamed afresh.

'Shall we set down a moment, take a little wine?' he went on. 'This is the Vintry, I think, so we should be well served.' His full lips twitched, in returning good humour. 'I can even ask a good-wife to stay by you as a companion, so your betrothed does not object.'

'I know very well where we are and I have no betrothed. I am a widow,' she responded tartly, seizing the chance to say it. Before he could say more she decided she would prove she was no fainting creature, lest he consider her soft. She seized the strut of an overhanging jetty with both arms, lifted herself away from him, swung and dropped neatly onto a house-step.

'Do you like wine?' she asked, as if what she had just done was the most natural thing in the world. Pride compelled her to add, 'I know where to find the best in London, especially the spiced sort.'

Silently he dismounted and strode alongside her where, with her standing on the step, their heads were exactly level. He looked kind again, and amused, and overall very much as if he longed to tweak her hair in its gold crespine.

His lips hovered so close to hers that she could smell his breath and see the tiny folds and creases of his mouth. Would he kiss her again? Should she kiss him?

He smiled instead, and offered her his arm. 'Well enough, Mistress Isabella, so lead on,' he said.

★   ★   ★

Isabella was an intriguing widow, Stephen decided, as they strolled beside the riverbank between the wharfs, passing a small skin of piment wine back and forth as they walked and talked. She was an enticing mixture of bold and shy — blushing easily but 'escaping' from his horse. She had a rich and varied knowledge of wine. The one she had suggested he buy, flavoured with cloves, ginger, honey and other spices, was very good. She had offered to pay for it, too, but he had refused at once.

'This is my suggestion, mistress, and I am glad to pay,' he told her and the smiling wine merchant, and he had not troubled to haggle, so content he had been with how the day was going.

'What is this called again?' he asked now, shaking the skin.

'Hippocras. Do you like it?'

'Very much.' He passed her the skin for the pleasure of watching her take a sip and of seeing her long white throat as she tipped back her head and swallowed. She had removed her gloves and he enjoyed seeing her slim, nimble fingers at work. She had the knack, too, which he had never mastered, of drinking from a wine-skin with delicacy, without spilling a drop.

'Are you a vintner's child?' he asked, picking up a stick and throwing it along the river-side path for his dog. His docile gray horse shook its mane but remained content to be simply led.

'Once, yes,' she replied, a curious answer which she clearly knew was odd because she at once began asking him about the court, who so-and-so was like and what Queen Philippa looked like.

He answered readily — no need to do other — and told her a little of his own work, pleased when she asked him questions concerning his craft. The creaking treadmill cranes of wine wharf were behind them by this time and they were closing on a group of women washing clothes by the water's edge when she stopped suddenly and turned about.

'We should go back. My family will be anxious.'

'Of course.' He offered his arm, which she did not take straight away, perhaps because she feared he would guess she was alarmed, but he could tell that already by the draining of color from her cheeks and lips.

She knows someone among those womenfolk and fears being recognized, but why? They are all maids, drab as sparrows. There is a mystery here, but it will keep until I know her better.

'Your husband was Richard?' he prompted, aware she had told him that earlier but wanting to keep conversation flowing and intrigued with what she might say. So far she had steered talk away from herself onto him.

'That's right. I married him at twelve.' She tucked her narrow hand through his arm and seemed as deliberately blithe as a skylark. 'A most trying age, I am told.'

'Seems too young to me,' he growled, sensing her comment had been used too often against her.

She colored a delicate rose. 'My husband, I mean Richard . . . he did wait until I was thirteen.'

Thirteen. My God. Poor little lass. What kind of man climbs into a maiden's bed when she is only thirteen? 'My Cecilia was closer to nineteen when we were wed.' He had been nineteen, a stripling, lanky as a young birch tree despite his labour in the forges, but merry then as a lark himself. 'We were together ten years.'

'And content as any couple taking home the Dunmore flitch,' Isabella observed shrewdly, referring to the custom in Essex of awarding a couple who had lived together a year without quarrelling a side or flitch of bacon.

'Aye, aye, we would have won that, had it been a custom of Kent,' he admitted, lost anew in memories until he heard her say quietly, 'We were not like that, Richard and me.'

One of the watermen of the river yelled something so coarse that, had the fellow been rowing closer, Stephen would have dragged him from his boat and thumped him. It had the virtue of making her laugh, at least.

'Was she very lovely?' she asked, and then shook her head, looking away from him to the barges on the river. 'Forgive me, I am wrong to pry.'

'Hush! She was beautiful and you worry too much.' He took her hand in his, glad he had removed his glove, and swung it as they walked. Her token, the small gold flower, was still snug in his other glove.

'Please, you must take me home. I shall be missed,' was all she said.

★   ★   ★

They moved swiftly then, to Isabella's relief. She had been disconcerted to see her mother's maid by the riverbank, but fortunately the maid had not approached her and Stephen seemed to have forgotten the entire incident. As he put her before him on his horse which, as Amice had said, truly was old, he was humming a tune.

'Yes, Ulysses is an antique, but nothing worries him,' he said, catching her looking. 'He is very good in processions and the like. Just as well,' he added innocently.

He mounted behind her and she could not think of a pert reply. Being cradled in his arms had been a floating, warm sensation, like a wonderful bath, and she had felt safe and protected. With him pressed against her — or was she against him? — she was conscious of him as a man. He was longer and harder in the body than Richard had been. She liked that, but despised the way she felt breathless, like a true maiden.

You cannot be stunned by his tanned good looks or the feel of his warm strong limbs. You must do enough, be available, or you will never see your son again.

'Shall I — ' She broke off before she uttered the fatal words *see you*, thereby betraying too desperate an interest. 'I mean, may I light a candle of thanks for your patron saint in my church? For your saving me,' she blundered on, wishing she could see his expression but not daring to turn for that would mean her thigh would brush along his. Each time Ulysses wandered into a pothole and his harness jangled, her body jangled lightly against Stephen's and she almost forgot to breathe.

She felt his breath stir the top of her head. 'Nay, I shall be lighting the candle, or rather my sister or daughter will do so on my behalf, for I have found you again.' He lifted one of her hands off the saddle pommel and raised it, kissing each finger. 'I am mightily glad I have, even if our reunion was a little unconventional.'

He has a daughter and he has told her about me. A mingled pleasure and pain lodged in her chest and she said quickly, 'I have a son, Matthew, but he is away for the present. What is your daughter called?'

'Joanna, after my mother. She is nine years old.' Isabella felt Stephen's long sigh right through her own body. 'With being at the court of the duke I do not see her as often as I would like, but I know she does well at my sister's. How old is your son?'

'Four years.'

Stephen started against her and she guessed he was frowning. 'That is

63

young to be away from his mother.'

'Yes it is.' She could say no more without fear of her voice cracking. *Does he think me a wicked mother? Perhaps I am, for I cannot have my son with me.*

They were approaching the back yards and gardens of the goldsmiths' houses, including that of her own, if she could call where she dwelt on sufferance a home.

She twisted about, the collision of their two bodies sending tiny sparks up and down her arms and legs. 'This is the place,' she said awkwardly, pointing to the stout stone wall around it and the stand of cherry and apple trees. 'I can go in here, by way of the small gate.'

She tried to dismount but he held her easily in place by means of an arm, gently but firmly. Instead he stepped down and came by his horse's flank to look up at her.

'This is the back of Richard Martinton's workshop. So you are his widow? I had heard the fellow was married.'

She nodded, wondering how Stephen had known Richard and whether he had liked him. It seemed unlikely from the little he had said and the tone of his deep voice. Many people had disliked her late husband, who was apt to be quarrelsome and spiteful, especially when drunk. Or worse, Richard might have owed Stephen money, or a favour, or betrayed him in some way.

Please, if this man loathed Richard, let him not loathe me.

Stephen was looking at her, studying her for so long she wondered if she had a smut on her cheek. 'That explains it,' he said cryptically. He stroked his horse's neck and she wished he might stroke her.

'You will be safe from here on? I would prefer to see you right indoors.'

'Oh no, I will be quite all right,' she said swiftly, aware that the longer they lingered the more likely a servant would report them to her mother-in-law. She did not want her 'family' questioning

Stephen, not yet. For the moment he was all hers.

Or is he?

Her mesh of thoughts broke and scattered as he dropped his horse's reins and lifted her straight into his arms. He held her aloft a moment, then slowly, inch by inch it seemed, he lowered her until they were face to face. 'Then I must let you go,' he said softly, his voice a growl.

'You should.' When he did not, she tried to move and her nose softly collided with his but otherwise she could not stir. Trapped in his iron grip, her feet dangling in the air, she bethought herself of a ruse, instead. 'I think I hear someone come.'

He grinned at her. 'I think you do not and even if you did, mistress, I would have an answer before I go.' He tightened his hold slightly.

'To what question?' she asked tartly, praying he would not notice how comfortable she felt within his arms, even with her feet dangling.

'Fool that I am, I forgot to ask!' He kissed her softly on the cheek. 'May I see you again, Isabella?'

Her spirits leapt up like a blazing fire. She knew that by all forms and manners she should not do it, but his lips were so close, so inviting. Feeling reckless, light-headed, her feet dangling, she kissed him gently on the mouth.

'I might take that as a yes?' he said, when her lips left his.

'Yes,' she responded, quelling a *please*.

'Good.' He kissed her in return but still he did not release her. Indeed he wove an arm beneath her bottom, so she was more securely supported. 'Was it by chance that you fell onto me?'

'What else?' she replied, hiding her face against his dark hair. She heard him chuckle and then somehow his lips were on hers again.

'However it was, or is, we should make a kiss of peace,' he murmured, his mouth claiming kiss after kiss.

'Stephen,' she began, unsure what

67

she would say, only wanting woman-like to be sure, to have a firm date, time and place so she could march into that den of her mother-in-law's and announce, 'He is seeing me *here* and *when* do I see Matthew?'

But Stephen deepened his kiss, stroking his lips along hers and easing his tongue into her mouth. She had never been kissed in such a way before, so close and intimate and warm. Her body responded, heating and softening against him. Before she knew it, her arms were around his neck and her tongue was exploring his mouth. He grunted a sharp exclamation of approval, bending her into his embrace.

'No more, or it shall not be enough.' Chuckling, he lowered her, touched the tip of her nose, kissed her face again and took a careful backward step. 'I must quarrel with you soon, if that is your kiss of peace.'

He mounted his small gray horse and cantered off, waving and calling, 'Until tomorrow!'

He was gone. Dazed, Isabella hugged herself and leaned against the garden wall, glad of a moment alone before she must face the family. So far, surely, so good. But had she done enough? Did that sweet, amazing kiss of peace mean more?

I should have asked him for a token, for Sir William may not believe me otherwise, she thought, but afterward she found herself smiling. Tomorrow would be her proof.

Tomorrow, and hopefully the day after that, and after that.

Then, please God, I shall see my son again.

4

'You will flirt and be pleasant — most pleasant — to other men. If you do not, you will never see Matthew again.' Sitting on the dais in the family great hall with his favourite jewel box placed on a small table beside him, Sir William fingered his gaudy costume and then the glittering inlays of the box. 'Do you understand?'

Torn between fury and despair, Isabella clenched her fists. 'No, I do not,' she answered, ignoring the hiss of displeasure from her mother-in-law, who stood alongside her on the hall tiles. 'I have done what you asked. I have secured Stephen's attention. I am winning his affections. He has a young daughter and I have my Matthew. They could be play-mates.'

Sir William picked his nose, a deliberate insult. Isabella heard the anger pounding in her ears, felt it prickle in her hands and feet. She longed to smash the heavily ornamented jewel box into her uncle's bored and haughty face. Hit him and keep on striking.

'Be quiet, girl,' muttered Margery, trying to seize her arm. Isabella whirled back. One part of her, the sensible Isabella, was clamoring for her silence. *Careful. If you speak too bluntly they will not let you visit Matthew.*

She thought of her son in his brave blue coat and spoke again, determined this time to wrest a concession from her tormentor.

'I do not understand why you have suddenly changed what I must do; changed it seems on a whim. I have done what you demanded. Now let me visit Matthew.'

Sir William yawned. 'Visit Matthew,' he mimicked. 'I grow weary of this complaint.'

Beside her, Margery, her mother-in-law, scowled afresh. 'You do not understand, girl. There is more than my grandson at stake here. We have the seals — '

'Not now, Margery,' warned Sir William, gripping the jewel box in clear alarm and irritation. Her mother-in-law fell silent at once.

Isabella remained fixed to the spot and refused to be diverted. 'Is it because I am being successful? Are you so petty?'

Sir William shrugged, swinging a leg as he settled more deeply into the master's chair. 'We have set our sights too low with Stephen Fletcher. You must aim higher.'

You did not expect me to win his interest so swiftly. Had Matthew been with her, Sir William's implied admission would have been gratifying. As it was, Isabella experienced a familiar frustration and a rising shame. 'Stephen is visiting me today. He is a good man, decent.' *And you cannot stand the idea of an honorable man being attracted to me, or of my being a little happy in his company.*

Sir William stroked his beard, then the jewel box, then his goldsmith's livery again. 'Go out with him, then. Take Mary and John with you.'

Isabella, guessing Sir William expected her to protest, slammed her teeth together and said nothing. Mary and John were her uncle's servants and spies in this house. Mary especially would report everything she did, or did not do, including how she behaved with Stephen and with other men. The idea of sour-faced, grasping Mary and her slack-bellied husband John being with her, watching her, listening to her conversations with Stephen was not to be borne. 'No,' she said.

Sir William snorted. 'You seem to think you have a choice.'

'Beat her.' Margery held up a broom. 'Beat her, teach her to obey.'

'Oh, no,' replied her kinsman, clearly enjoying the moment as he smoothed and tweaked his beard a second time. 'We have done that before, cousin, and the wretch learns nothing. No, I shall not touch her.'

He smiled. 'I will beat Matthew instead.'

'Do not — You must not!' Isabella ran at him but a scream from her mother-in-law had three servants, including John, rushing into the hall. Before she could touch or even argue with Sir William, the three men grabbed her, John slapping his hand across her mouth with such force that she saw stars and her teeth rattled.

'Remove her,' said Sir William, with a languid wave of his hand. 'She knows what she must do.' Abruptly his face and manner hardened. 'Get the mewling bitch out of my sight.'

Isabella was hauled away.

★　★　★

Riding from his sister's house, Stephen told himself that it was good his daughter Joanna was at ease and sleeping through the night. He told himself it was good that work at the forges went well. He told himself —

No. No more telling. It has been seven days now and Isabella is different. I do not understand what has happened, but she is no longer easy with me.

He could not believe that she had changed in her feelings toward him. They had begun so well. Yet, the very day after he had caught her, saved her and taken her home, the very next day after they had kissed, she had visibly cooled in her manner to him. At the same time yet more weight had dropped from her so she looked older. Even her bright gold hair seemed dulled.

She always agrees to meet me, yet is subdued in my company. At times I see her looking at nothing, as if staring at something else.

Yesterday he had asked her bluntly what troubled her. 'Nothing, 'tis only a stomach-ache,' she had answered, glancing at the two servants who were always with her these days, a mildewed-looking pair. And today, when he had planned to take her to his home to visit his daughter she had cried off, saying she must work. Then, contrary-wise, she had begged him to visit her in the evening. 'We might spend time with my friend Amice the spice-seller, at her home.' She had then added in a lower voice, 'Amice knows Matthew, too.'

'Agreed,' Stephen had said at once, for he wanted answers. Perhaps, away from her family and the miserable servants who shadowed her every step, Isabella would be disposed to supply them.

What is she about? The only times she had been truly animated had been when she spoke of her son and when she questioned him closely about Kent and the houses and villages there, asking for the names of the land-owners. *What has gone wrong for her? Why does she not tell me? Why are those servants always with her?*

It did not matter to him that he and

Isabella scarcely knew each other or had only just met. It did not matter that she was less charming. His sister, had she known, would have scolded that he wasted his time, but Stephen sensed there was more to Isabella's contradictory behavior than a simple change of heart. He was determined to discover more, and he was becoming increasingly determined to win her. He knew she was in trouble, in pain, and he longed to help her — if she would let him.

Stephen meanwhile was aware that he was filling in time before their next meeting that evening. He had played hide-and-seek with Joanna, mended a trestle leg for his sister, and spent several hours at the royal armories. Now he took a wherry to the Savoy, the palace of his lord Henry, the Duke of Lancaster, to discuss a commission of armor for the duke.

The king of France was staying at the Savoy as an honored prisoner and hostage. Duke Henry wished the king's stay to be as pleasant as possible and, as he was admitted through the riverside gate to the palace, Stephen was not surprised to see the whole place busy.

The duke, it turned out, could not see him that day. Returning by way of the rose garden back to the river, Stephen reflected on the wishes of the powerful and lamented having to leave his daughter Joanna for a wasted journey. Still, it was a bright, sunny day and had his mood been less distracted he would have smiled at the brightly-garbed figures, strolling along the graveled walks. *I must bring Isabella and her son here, with Joanna. And why have I not met Matthew? There is some mystery there.*

'I will not do that.'

His train of thought interrupted, Stephen turned, seeing only a wall of huge rosebushes, not yet in flower. Whoever had protested was behind that living screen.

'No! I said no. I shall be no man's plaything.'

The anger in the young woman's voice had Stephen pushing his way through the thorns.

Through the other side of the great rosebush he half-expected to see a maid struggling with a gallant but to his utter shock he found Isabella instead. Her surly servants were remonstrating with her, both at once, the maid hanging onto her arm to keep her between them.

'You must, for 'tis what Sir William ordered,' the maid was saying.

While the man added, 'You know we must make reports. If you do not do this we are all undone.'

Stephen stepped closer. 'Release my lady at once,' he ordered. 'Away with you!'

The servants took one look at his face and fled, hurrying off in the direction of the vegetable gardens. Stephen remained where he was, rooted to the spot. Relief and anger warred in him. He unclenched his fists and Isabella flinched.

'You need not cringe from me,' he said quietly. He had not meant to say more but somehow the accusation slipped out. 'You told me you were working.'

Isabella did not blush. She said nothing, but backed off and turned to follow her servants. She had lost still more weight, he noted, and though her dress and shoes were neat, her hair was spurting out of its net in a foaming cloud and her eyes were as mad as a berserker's. She looked wild, and dangerous.

'Wait.' He strode after her, going past her and barring her way. 'Why are you here? You told me you were working.'

'I lied.' She hurled the words while staring beyond him, looking ready to claw her way through more than thorns. 'I lie, Stephen, do you not know that yet? But you must let me go. I must catch Mary and John, else all is lost.'

She darted to one side to lunge by him but Stephen was faster. He caught her hand in his. 'I know a short-cut. This way.'

He was helping when she had expected him to berate her or worse, to stop her altogether. Panting and with her heart and feet pounding, Isabella followed Stephen, putting her faith in him even after he had realized she had played him false. They ran past a kitchen block and a workshop with a thatched roof and then scrambled through a small postern to the great street of the Strand outside. A swift glance in both directions told her that, short-cut or not, they were too late. Mary and John were nowhere in sight.

Too breathless to moan she sank to her knees and rocked herself. *It is over. Mary and John will rush to Sir William and tell him everything. Tell him I refused. I will never see Matthew again.* A keening wail built in her throat and her chest tightened further, her vision darkening as the shadow of her fate overwhelmed her.

'None of that.' Stephen lifted her up,

snapped his fingers at a lingering musician with a viol. With the blood still hammering in her chest and ears, Isabella did not hear what he said to the lad but he turned her toward the river. 'We take a boat and out-run them that way.'

'Why?' she gasped, when she could speak.

Stephen did not pretend to misunderstand her. 'Because I care and I can and I never liked your waste of a husband or his kin.' His face was as keen as a blade. 'Now do you come or do I carry you?'

'Run,' she wheezed, ignoring the stitch in her side. 'Hurry.' She lurched from his arms and staggered a few steps.

In an ungainly mass of whirling legs and arms they rushed back to the river, Isabella jumping so recklessly into the waiting wherry that the whole boat rocked furiously and the waterman cursed her.

'Save your breath and row,' ordered

Stephen, coming alongside her. 'Row to London, man, and hurry!'

He sprawled beside her, catching his breath a moment, then took her hand again. 'Tell me,' he said. 'Tell me it all.'

She glanced at the ferryman, reluctance and eagerness flickering across her face like the reflections of the water skimming beneath them. Stephen lowered his head. 'Whisper to me,' he said.

'Or pay me double to keep quiet and shout it,' said the waterman with a grin.

Doubtful as a hind approaching a baited trap, Isabella leaned away from both of them.

'You need help,' Stephen said steadily. From all his time spent in the forge and the armories he sensed that this was the moment of decision between them. Isabella would share her truth fully with him now or they would not truly meld together. He tipped up her chin. Her face was as gray as the weather was bright. 'I want to help you.'

She leaned into him, against his

shoulder. 'We do not know each other,' she whispered.

'We know enough of each other.'

'We met only a few days past, not even a month ago.'

She argued even while she was pressed up against him and unconsciously sought comfort and counsel. Her wariness was one of habit, not desire, Stephen guessed. He put his arm about her. 'Does that matter?' he asked. 'You are a woman of London and the world. I am sure you understand my character most clearly.'

Isabella said nothing but Stephen felt her settle into the crook of his arm. *Her body trusts me so that is a start.* The ferryman was occupied with navigating their wherry through the arches of London Bridge, a tricky, dangerous maneuver, especially for a single waterman, and one to which he bent all his attention. Isabella watched him and closed her eyes, her limbs becoming as taut as harp strings.

Tense, and not only because of

getting past the bridge. The stakes are high here and I believe I know why. Nothing else makes sense.

'Shall I say what I think?' said Stephen softly, keeping his eyes on her. 'Richard Martinton's family keep your son. I know he does not live with you in London. You speak of him with such longing.'

Isabella screwed up her eyes and made a small choking sound.

'You asked after places and house-holders in Kent. Martinton's kin have property in Kent. I know because the family is notorious in those parts. They are not well-liked.'

Isabella looked at him. 'What can I say?'

'Your keepers are not with you here. You need not fear my telling them anything. I want to help.'

She continued to watch him, the question *why* now urgent in her face. 'I may lose even what I have,' she said, cautious still.

'But what is that, really? Do they

keep promising that your son will be with you and reneging on that promise?' A new suspicion flared in his mind. 'What do they want you to do, Isabella?'

She stared beyond him, her pinched, gray face blooming into a brighter crimson, like a molten rod of iron. Shame, he surmised, and anger.

'Your kin see me as a means to win favor at court?' He asked the question very quietly, tempering his own rage.

'Yes,' whispered Isabella. 'But they guessed I liked you, too.'

'And that changed things?' he asked gently, reining in his temper again.

The shadow of the arches of London Bridge hid her face but he felt Isabella give a small nod. 'For me it changed everything,' she admitted. She hunched into a tighter ball beside him, misery pouring off her like smoke from a furnace. 'They wanted more. They always want more. I was told to flirt with others, to draw the attentions of other men.' Her voice dropped lower still. 'To become mistress to many men.'

And Isabella had said no, Stephen thought, recalling her stalwart protests in the gardens of the Savoy palace.

'Or I lose Matthew forever.' She was as pale as a corpse, her eyes distant mirrors and memories of pain. 'Now you can destroy me, if you choose,' she continued, in the same dull, dead voice.

I always knew Richard Martinton and his clan deserved to burn in hell. Let me send a few of them there, though I'll swing for it. The burst of anger was cleansing but the disgust that followed was as dark as slag. *To abuse a mother so . . . this family is beyond contempt.*

He plunged a fist into the cold river, quenching his rage as their bobbing little boat burst through shadows into sunlight again and the ferryman relaxed on his sculls. He did not waste his time on being offended by Isabella's confession that she had sought him out. Thoughts on that score were luxuries now that their waterman was sculling swiftly to the nearest wharf. In another moment they would be running again. 'Yet why should we run?' he asked aloud.

'I must be there to put my side, to defend myself.'

He shook his head. 'Has it made any difference in the past? Ignore them, Isabella, be free of them. Take their dungeon out of your head.'

She stared at him, a stunned blankness in her eyes. He did not know if he was reaching her or not but he knew he had to keep trying. *This is the moment.*

'Can we speak freely at your friend's house?'

'At Amice's? Yes, but I must return before John and Mary — '

He cut across her. 'Your kin will believe whatever that greasy pair tell them, so why the haste? We can do more out of doors. Once you are back you will be spied on and stopped. You will be in their power again.'

'I am always in their grip,' Isabella spat. 'You cannot understand, you are a man. You have nothing to lose.'

That stung Stephen. 'You are wrong. My wife is dead.'

'But you have your daughter!' Isabella struck her breastbone with her fingers. 'Joanna is yours. My son is not mine. Can you not understand? I do not even know where he is!'

Tearing herself from his embrace she stood up in the wherry and in another instant would have hurled herself onto the nearest quayside. Stephen snatched her back, holding her wrists with such force that he could feel the narrow, fragile bones grind beneath his fingers as she struggled. Her sudden fierceness surprised him, but only for a moment.

If she is an angel, can she not be an avenger also? She has been badly wronged.

Still, however much her furious beauty stirred him he dared not release her.

'Lively one there,' the waterman chortled, as Stephen man-handled Isabella ashore and paid their fare. 'Mind how you go.'

5

He remembered where her friend had looked from the upper window on *The Street* and soon found her shop without any directions from his companion. Hand in hand, hurrying beside him, Isabella was silent but he did not make the mistake of believing she was resigned. 'How are you?' he asked, as they sped along the alleyways to the spice seller's.

'Thinking,' she answered.

* * *

All my life I have been taught to obey. I obeyed my parents when they told me to marry Richard. I did everything my husband's kin asked of me. Richard beat me, but not because I rebelled against him. He did so because he wanted to see me broken and sniveling.

90

It amused him to watch me cringe.

Stephen is not like that.

I obeyed my father and he cast me off. I obeyed my husband and he beat me. I obeyed my husband's family and they took my son. They hide him and speak most carefully in my hearing so I cannot work out where he is. They take away my money and jewels so I have no means, no power of discovery. They consider my opinions and wishes worthless.

Stephen is not like that.

'You are a woman of London and the world,' he had said, and 'You need not cringe from me.' Best of all, 'I never liked your waste of a husband or his kin,' and 'I want to help you.'

He was right, too. When had her arguments or pleas made any difference? She had obeyed and had never been granted a single wish. *What is the point of my being a good daughter, wife, or daughter-in-law when it makes no difference? When I do not get what I want?*

She was alone. She had always been alone, apart from when she had Matthew. Yesterday, even an hour ago she had considered her solitude a curse and a weakness. Now she looked at the world with new eyes and saw her singularity as strength.

I do not have to obey any of them. They truly have no power over me.

What had Stephen said? 'Has it made any difference in the past?' No it had not, of course it had not. She had groveled to win any glimpse of Matthew, she had sold everything she owned to be given time with her son and she had not even been granted that, only a brief sight of him from the back, not even his face.

Be free of them, Stephen had said. Take their dungeon out of your head.

It was a revelation.

For all that I must hurry. I do not want my son beaten or hurt. We must hurry . . .

★ ★ ★

Isabella's friend Amice unbarred the back door to her shop and bustled them inside. The beautiful, dark-skinned woman asked no questions but swept them past her wide-eyed apprentice and up into a narrow upstairs chamber, closing the downstairs shutters on her spices and telling her apprentice to check stores instead.

'We are losing you customers,' Stephen remarked when the spice-seller returned in a swirl of red, rustling silks and a savor of vanilla and cinnamon.

'Not important.' Amice handed him a steaming cup of raspberry tisane and knelt beside the chair where he had guided Isabella to sit. 'Has she had bad news of Matthew?' Amice demanded, looking closely at the small, still figure.

Isabella stirred at her scrutiny. 'No news, never any news.' She smiled and stroked Amice's dark hair. 'But I am thinking, beloved. Finally I am thinking.'

Amice pressed a cup of tisane into Isabella's unresisting hand and motioned with her eyes to the threshold. Stephen put his cup on the window ledge and cleared his throat. 'I must seek your privy.'

'I will show you,' said Amice.

'I dare not leave Issa for long,' she added at once, as she and Stephen clattered down the stairs again. 'What has happened?'

He told what he knew in a few choice words. Lingering in her tiny back yard, constantly glancing up the stairs, Amice snorted when he explained what Isabella had admitted.

'She has not told a peppercorn's worth of it! Issa has been bullied for years, starved, beaten, left to rot in the heart of this city during the pestilence and her son forcibly taken from her. Richard Martinton was a pig. I wanted to stick a blade in him myself.'

Stand in line, Stephen thought. Anger made him light-headed, with a dragging thirst. 'Her parents? Can they do nothing?'

Amice curled her lower lip. 'More useless sacks of offal. Issa's father is a vintner, did she tell you that?'

Stephen nodded but got no chance to reply.

'Did she say that her own father sent her to that pig Martinton when she was twelve? Aged twelve!'

'Yes, she told me.'

'Did she? You must have won some of her confidence for Issa to admit anything. Did she also tell you that she was the bride meant to stop a blood feud? Last year when Martinton lurched from her bed and clubbed down one of her father's men it was Issa who was blamed and beaten. Beaten by his family and blamed by her own, I might add. Her parents now ignore her in the street. Even if the Martintons allowed it, they would not have Issa back with them.'

'A brawl last year? How can they blame Isabella for that?' Stephen stared at the roof-tops of London, trying to bar from his mind the image of his gold-haired, falling angel being struck, of being rejected and ignored by her parents, the very people who should have loved her. He failed, the dark knowledge an evil to him. 'Married off at twelve,' he repeated, and shook his head in disbelief, shocked afresh. He thought only the nobility worked that kind of carelessness with girls. His Cecilia was eighteen, almost nineteen when they were married. Amice's Issa, his Isabella, had been a child herself.

'Made to marry. Wedded, bedded, beaten and discarded.'

'We must find her son, get him back to her.' Stephen was aware of far more that was due to Isabella but this was the first.

'And then?' Amice challenged, her fine eyes as bright as a bird's. 'The law of this land makes the boy Martinton's, or his kin's. They may have shipped him to France for all we know.'

'I will speak to the prince, to my lord,' Stephen said, with a growing certainty. He had influence and access and Isabella would finally have protection. *I will protect her.*

'My husband's kindred wanted more than they assumed you would be able to get them,' said Isabella, standing perilous at the top of the stairs, as slender as a candle flame. 'When you showed yourself willing to court me they instantly decided to be more ambitious. They are goldsmiths after all and their guild is notorious for its pride.'

Amice hissed in a long breath and opened her arms, as if afraid her friend would tumble down the steps. 'Issa, why not go sit down again?'

'I will not fall, Amice.' She smiled at her friend and looked at him. 'They call you a blacksmith, Stephen, and they do not mean it well, but to me smiths are the heart of every place there is.'

Her generous words made him catch his breath but only for an instant. 'I began as a smith, and am proud to be so.' Stephen was more but he gladly claimed the title . . . *the heart of every place there is.* Humbled, inspired, he walked to the head of the staircase, wishing Isabella would return to the upper chamber, longing to sweep her safe into his arms. He took a step up on the stair.

'Do not be troubled, Stephen. I shall not fall again.'

'I believe you.' He did, for she looked as steady as an angel.

'I have thought, Stephen. For years I could not, because of fear and constant trouble. You showed me the space and the way to free myself. Because of those things I have thought. Blacksmiths have a guild, have they not?'

Stephen blinked at the question, wondering where this strange conversation was going. 'I am in the guild of armorers,' he began, 'and I know many smiths.'

'And blacksmiths are in every village. Places of gossip and news, places where the comings and goings of strangers and worthies are discussed.'

'I agree.' What she said made sense. 'Yet I am sorry to say that I do not know every blacksmith in Kent.'

Isabella swayed and alarmed, he took another step upward toward her.

'Do not be concerned,' she said, recovering, gripping the door jamb. 'I am quite clear-headed, for the first time in years, I might add.'

'For God, Issa, sit down on the steps,' pleaded Amice.

'Let us all sit,' said Stephen and he did so, settling on the narrow treads, another step closer to Isabella. 'I do know a great many smiths, including several of Kent,' he went on, to hearten her. 'I can get word out to ask after your boy.'

His cantering heartbeat slowed when Isabella copied him and sat down on the top step. Amice came alongside him. 'That might work,' she said softly. 'The fellowship of craftsmen and all. Will they be discreet?'

'They will if I ask them to be.' Stephen said. He turned again to Isabella. 'I will begin today,' he promised. 'It should not take long.'

'Are you certain you wish to begin this, my lord?'

Isabella's formal question startled him and he frowned, considering the matter settled. 'What do you mean?'

Her steady gaze on him faltered and she glanced down at her knees. 'I mean that Richard's family . . . they like to have a hostage to use.' She hugged her knees and rocked back and forth on the step. 'You and your daughter lodge with your sister, do you not? And you mentioned that her husband is away at sea?'

It fitted, Stephen thought, while he heard Amice softly cursing in some exotic tongue. *Isabella is right. I need them away from the house now, or Bedelia and Joanna will be used as hostages.*

His heart clenched at the thought and he suddenly understood far more clearly the oppression Isabella had been enduring. *This cannot go on.*

He twisted about to Amice. 'Your apprentice, is he reliable?'

'He is slow and a touch idle, plays on his limp at times, but I would say yes.'

'Then he can take a message and a token of mine to my sister's.' Bedelia might be bossy but she had sense. He would write the note in the secret script they had made up between them as youngsters, so she understood the urgency and danger. 'Bedelia knows to go to Thomas Smith's house in case of trouble. He is a fellow armorer.'

'Send the message now,' said Isabella, chewing on her lower lip. 'I would have no one else threatened because of me and mine.' Her voice cracked. 'I could not, cannot bear that.'

'As soon as we are done here,' Stephen replied, with a steadiness he did not quite feel. 'Get my sister and daughter safe, yes, but we need some idea of where to search for Matthew before we go rushing off. Anything, Isabella, any clue.'

'I must hurry.' Isabella inclined her head. Her eyes still gleamed but she looked less haunted. 'I have thought of something else,' she said. 'Richard's family never told me anything but as I served and cleared up after them I overheard a great deal.' Her voice caught. 'Soon after . . . soon, when Matthew and I were parted, Sir William spoke of a place of devilry, an orchard where Satan had left his footprint.'

Amice crossed herself. Stephen leaned closer.

'I think Sir William knew I was listening,' Isabella went on, 'for he jested that my son would not find the fruit there to his liking.'

'Pig!' Amice muttered.

Stephen agreed but for him anger was overwhelmed by exultation. 'Well-remembered, Isabella, and more than enough for a Kentish man like me,' he said, with a grim smile.

He watched her stop breathing and lean forward, willing him to say more, her face bright, her eyes like living flames. He was most happy to do so. 'There is no need for me to send word to the blacksmiths. I already know where your son is being held. Satan's footprint is an old story in Kent.'

'So where?' demanded Amice.

'The village of Newington, close to the old Roman road.' Stephen rose to his feet. 'I can have us there in less than a day.' He grinned, some of the tension falling off his shoulders. 'The farriers and smiths will loan us good horses along the way, if need be, as part of that fellowship of blacksmiths Amice mentioned.'

Isabella jumped to her feet and flew down the stairs to him. 'Thank you, how can I thank you?' she gabbled, hugging him with surprising strength. 'I am coming!' she shouted with such force that the staircase rattled.

'We are,' said Stephen and Amice together, both of them caught as Isabella was, between laughter and tears.

★   ★   ★

Isabella did not see the countryside passing as she rode out from London. Stephen insisted she ride behind him and she was glad to do so. Amice, changed into a man's tunic and hood, might pass for a striking youth as she handled her spirited roan with the casual ease of a knight, but Isabella was less certain of her abilities, especially now.

I am about to see Matthew.

She could think of nothing else. Even Stephen's reassuring bulk seemed as insubstantial as smoke. She clung to him, her arms tight about his waist, her cheek pressed firmly against his back, and wished only to go faster.

'Will Matthew be pleased to see me? I have no gift for him. Will he have grown? Will he know me? Will he like me? Will he like my gown? I wish I had something for him.'

She did not realize she was speaking aloud until she had an answer.

'He will love you,' Stephen called, above the pounding of the horses' hooves. 'He will brag to all his friends of your beauty.'

I pray so. Stephen's extravagant

claims still comforted her and she inhaled his musky scent, glad she rode behind him and not Amice, feeling him moving with the snorting horse.

They stopped at a forge on the Roman road to feed and water the horses. Stephen suggested she take a brief walk with Amice while he spoke to the farrier. 'I took your suggestion, Isabella, and went with it,' he added with a smile.

While she and Amice wandered, Isabella staring always at the road ahead of them, at the large skies of scudding clouds, a carpenter suddenly ran out from a lean-to workshop.

'Black demon and whore! Get away!'

More startled than shocked they faltered, Isabella keeping a sharp eye on the saw in fellow's left hand, but Stephen was the quickest. In a few long strides he stepped between them.

'For God, man, leave off your bullying of these good womenfolk.' He caught the carpenter's raised hand, stopping it and the saw in a grip of steel. 'Go back to your shop and drink no more today.'

The carpenter gawped and worked his mouth until words spewed out. 'They y'orn?'

'Under my protection and that of my guild.' Stephen removed the saw from the smaller man. 'Come, I shall walk you back.'

They disappeared into the lean-to and a few moments Stephen reappeared, to the sound of furious sawing. He went first to Amice.

'I am sorry for that,' he said, taking her hand in his, smiling down at her with his eyes. 'That a man of Kent should be so ignorant.'

With a regal gesture, Amice waved it aside. 'I have had worse in London. Are we good to go?'

Stephen nodded, glancing at the larger thatched building beside the lean-to. Eyes blinked back at them from the smoky gloom of the ale-house. 'Aye, it be best.'

'Amice,' Isabella began, sorry and

ashamed for the trouble she was causing, but her friend shook her head. 'This place smells wrong now.'

They moved out quickly.

★ ★ ★

Stephen felt exposed on the Roman road and glad to canter off it as soon as they were out of sight of the hamlet. He drew rein beneath a blossoming apple orchard and stepped down, passing a flask to Amice as she also drew rein.

'I know the way to Newington blindfolded from here,' he told them. I will take us by old track ways and green paths so we may reach the village unnoticed.'

'Good,' said Isabella, glancing at the cloudy sky to check the position of the sun. 'We should hurry.'

'We shall be there long before sunset,' Stephen reassured her though he wondered at her insistence on speed. *Amice promises me her apprentice will deliver my message to Bedelia, so my daughter and sister are now safe at Tom's and out of harm's reach of the wretched Martinton clan. We ourselves are way ahead of any pursuit or news from her in-laws. What else does she fear?*

'That will be a blessing,' Amice murmured and she hid her face behind the flask. She had been a little subdued since her rude encounter with the carpenter, which was scarcely surprising.

Isabella slid off his horse and went straight to her friend. She touched Amice's stirrup. 'I am so sorry for this, for the trouble I am causing.'

'No,' said Amice at once, more forcefully, speaking for Stephen, too. 'A pig of a carpenter is not your fault, Issa. Your pigs of in-laws are not your fault.'

'Believe her.' Stephen said quietly.

Isabella turned and stumbled toward the trees, muttering about needing to make water. Amice lowered the flask. 'If you hurt her, master armorer, I shall have your hide. That is one reason I have come on this venture. Just so we understand each other.'

Stephen smiled at her vehemence. 'She has loyal friends.'

'Isabella tended me during the pestilence. Everyone else, including my apprentice, fled in fear. Issa kept coming. Hers is a quiet courage.' Amice gave a quick grin, her eyes very bright. 'A little fever laid me out but we did not know that until later. It could have been the plague.'

'Pity she did not pass it to her relations,' Stephen growled.

Amice laughed out loud. 'I like you, master armorer! Help us get Matthew for her and I will love you forever.'

'I will do that gladly,' Stephen said. *And if I can bring the smiles back to my Mistress Angel's face I shall do that, too.*

*   *   *

As Stephen foretold, they reached the village of Newington a good hour before sunset. Spotting the church tower, he suggested that Isabella and Amice stay back in a small wood until he had scouted about the place. 'I shall visit the forge, discover the news,' he said. 'I will say my wife has a little boy and ask if there are any children hereabouts who might be his playmates.'

'That is fine,' Amice agreed, eyes gleaming.

Isabella also thought it good but could not help adding, 'You will be quick? And take care?'

'Both, Mistress Angel,' came back his cheerful reply and then he cantered off.

Isabella fretted in the wood while the horses browsed the hawthorn bushes and Amice scoured beneath the trees for orchids. Hope warred with despair in her so that when she heard a lively horse galloping toward them she rushed from cover, too anxious to be prudent and wait to see who was coming.

★   ★   ★

'A hearty welcome!' Stephen reined in, leaned down and lifted her onto his saddle before him. He kissed her for the joy of seeing her again. He kissed her again so she would keep him in mind when they had her child safe. He kissed her a third time because he had great news. 'I have learned of and seen the house we want, my dear, and a small boy in a blue tunic is playing with whip and top outside it even now.'

Isabella paled and tried to scramble off his mount. Guessing her intent, Stephen coiled an arm about her narrow waist.

'No lass, we shall be quicker on horseback.' He could feel her trembling, heard her hiccup of surprise and tension. 'Come,' he went on gently, 'Let us ride and rescue your son.'

6

Their ride was over in moments. Isabella felt as if the crown of her head were exploding and light flooding through her. She saw the small, brave figure playing in the street ahead of them and feared for an instant that it was a dream. *So often I have woken from this lovely hope and found the nightmare goes on.*

She started as Stephen lifted her from the horse and set her gently on the ground. She felt a breeze tug at her collar and watched it ruffle the soft baby curls of the small, fair-haired boy who played on the house-step, now only feet away from her. She took a step nearer, then another step, certain and at the same time wanting to be absolutely sure . . .

He was still there, still wonderfully real. A small, fair-haired boy dressed in a creased blue tunic, sitting with a forgotten whip and top beside him as he doodled in the dust. *My little boy.*

'Matthew,' she croaked. Intent on his drawing, he had not seen or heard her yet. She drank him in as a man that is dying of thirst will fall upon a sparkling fountain: his long, trembling eyelashes, the sweet infant curve of his forehead, his long, narrow arms and legs. *He will be tall, like his father, but nothing like Richard in nature.*

I wish I had a gift for him.

She did not realize she had spoken aloud until she felt a warm hand on her shoulder.

'Here,' said Stephen softly. He offered her the gold and silver flower that he had caught from her hand when she had floated in the golden cage above *The Street* in London. 'I would have been sorry to lose it, for 'tis a lovely thing,' he went on, smiling down at her, his gray-green eyes a sea of feeling, 'but will gladly give it to your son.' He twirled the jewel, the glints of

113

gold shining across his face.

'Thank you,' she whispered.

He put the trinket in her palm but she could not hold anything right now and it slipped through her nerveless fingers. The flashing bauble fell to the ground, brighter still as the sun broke through the clouds.

Matthew must have spotted the sparkle for he looked round. His eyes widened. 'Mamma,' he said, and laughed. He rose to his feet on unsteady, heron-thin legs and held up his arms to be picked up and gathered in. 'My mamma.'

Isabella flew to him.

* * *

Sitting on the house-step, Matthew and Isabella were at last united. The boy was in his mother's arms and lap, holding up his fingers to be kissed one by one. Isabella rocked him, crooning a lullaby. Her face, transfigured by exultation, shone brighter than the sun

114

so she was as gold and blue as any Madonna, sun, moon and stars in one. She wept and laughed, at one point swinging Matthew up off her knee to show him to the world. 'My boy, my beautiful boy.'

Stephen knelt to this miracle and was swept into it, Isabella flinging an arm around his shoulders, weeping and laughing against his chest. He kissed her and Matthew, delighting with them, wishing his daughter were here, so she could join in.

'Ami!' Matthew held up his arms again.

Coming up rapidly to join them, Amice swung the child into her embrace, standing beside Isabella and stroking her friend's golden hair. 'All done, all safe,' she was saying, over and over. As Isabella shuddered, Amice crouched to release Matthew, who toddled instantly back to his mother.

'Hurry,' Amice hissed against Stephen's back, and he nodded. He knew they were too visible, that at any instant there could be a shout, a warning to the Martinton household, but how could he interrupt this reunion?

Thank God the villagers are at their suppers so they do not see. It was surely part of a larger neglect that Matthew was not at supper, was even unattended, but right now that was a blessing. Newington, too, like other English places since the pestilence, had fewer souls to keep watch.

Besides, there was no need to hurry his golden girl. With her little boy riding on her hip Isabella pushed herself from the step and began to walk steadily back toward the wood where she and Amice had waited for him.

'Look at her!' Amice hissed, with a jab of an urgent finger. 'Sees nothing but Matthew, strolls as if she is in heaven already, sails straight past the backside of my roan who kicks like a mule. Has she noticed that I have brought the horses? Have you?'

'I grudge her nothing.' He could hear her singing another lullaby.

116

'She is not safe for human company.'

'Not yet.' Stephen smiled. 'She will be.'

* * *

He wanted to hasten back to London, hug Joanna close and shelter all of them within Thomas's house, but instinct warned him that Isabella needed peace and time with her son. A roadside inn was too risky, with too many people who might remember them if Sir William's men came searching — as they surely would.

'A religious house will take us for tonight,' Isabella said serenely, when Stephen, striding beside his horse with Isabella and Matthew riding, tried to speak quietly to Amice on the matter. She was right, of course.

'Alms for the monks will buy us silence, too,' remarked Amice. She was right as well.

'Agreed.' Stephen knew of a small monastery that they could reach easily before nightfall. He squeezed Isabella's foot and she smiled at him, haloed by the evening sunset. *Already she looks less thin. I know that to be impossible, but still, there it is. The brightness has returned in her, because she has her son.* He hoped, too, a little brightness was for him.

'Tell them you are married,' Amice said, with a knowing glance at her friend. 'They will put you together in a guest room.'

Isabella blushed. She kissed her son's downy hair as Matthew dozed before her in the saddle, but said nothing.

Besieged by images of himself and Isabella in a bed, Stephen cleared his throat. 'We should all stay together. It will be safer.'

But mark this, Isabella did not object. He did not object, either.

★ ★ ★

Still he was patient. He wanted her — how he wanted her! — but instinct told him to rein in, be still. *She has been months without her son. Nothing else must come between them.* His desires must wait.

The monks welcomed them, fed them a supper of leek porry and fish and put them in a guest chamber with a great four-poster bed that could sleep all four of them. At once, Amice claimed the bed space closest to the doorway. 'I like to be able to move at night, in bed and out of it,' she said.

Stephen noted how she did not quite look at Isabella as she spoke and felt his heart expand with gratitude. He nodded thanks to her as Amice took her place beside the door, preparing to sleep in her clothes.

'Then I do not have to dress again when we rise for the midnight services,' she said, and shrugged. 'You may choose to do differently.'

'I will stay as I am,' said Isabella quickly.

'Goodnight,' Amice called and instantly rolled over.

'Goodnight, my friend, and thank you.' Isabella bedded down beside Amice, her son cradled in her arms. She looked up and Stephen's heart raced afresh as he saw her eyes. 'Are you for bed, St . . . Stephen?' she stammered, shyly patting the mattress in invitation.

'I am.' He settled next to her, with the monastery stone wall at his back. Isabella in her creased gown and her blonde tresses unruly on the pillow had never looked more delicious, more kissable. He did not want to roll away from her, but still . . . Keeping his eyes fixed on her, Stephen reversed in the bed and forced his reluctant body right up to the cold stones, willing their chill into his loins.

Matthew, after demanding and receiving a night-time story from Isabella, slept quickly. Stephen watched her watching him and was surprisingly content.

She has her child. Now I must ensure she keeps him. Whatever happens between us, I must do this. As a mother, as herself, Isabella deserves no less. Pray God I can do this.

If he failed, she might forgive, but he would never forgive himself.

7

Isabella was sleeping after the early service. Beside her, Matthew played with her hair and the silver and gold flower that Stephen had retrieved from the dust and handed again to his mother. Now, dropping a kiss onto the boy's head, trailing a hand over Isabella's shoulder, Stephen eased himself off the great bed and slipped out of the chamber into the dawn.

He stood in the yard, looking at the great monastery church, and listened to the birds and the silences between their calls. He drew in a large breath, inhaling the smells of his childhood — the sea, the blossom, the green earth. *How have I forgotten this?* He had a small-holding in Kent, close to the coast. It was time, and perhaps safer, to take his family down there, take Joanna and his sister *and Isabella and Matthew, if Isabella will come.*

A whiff of spices told him that Amice had entered the yard. She wasted no words in greeting. 'What next?'

Stephen half-turned, glad to speak to Isabella's closest friend. The matter had kept him awake all last night. 'If I ask her, will she take me?'

'Ginger and pepper! Have you not noticed how she looks at you, man?'

'But after her first marriage, is it too soon?'

Amice clicked her tongue, as if impatient. 'Do you love her?'

Stephen smiled.

'Then ask!'

'It will be safer for her and Matthew,' he added, trying to be practical and sensible. Sensing a change in the air behind him, Stephen looked round. Isabella was standing on the threshold, Matthew riding on her hip.

Amice moved first. 'I will take Matt,' she said, holding out her arms to the chuckling little boy. 'Go, walk in the cloister or something. You two have things you need to say to each other. Go on.'

Seeing nothing but Isabella, Stephen held out his hand to her. Please accept me, his heart thundered. *Please.*

Her warm little fingers wrapped round his. 'I know the way,' she said. 'Follow me.'

★ ★ ★

The cloister was quiet, the rising sun beating down on a single gardener and some drowsy bumblebees. Isabella sat beside a narrow pillar and looked out over the herbs and flowers. She felt Stephen crouch beside her, still clutching her hand.

She glanced at him and the world stopped. The ardor in his lean, tanned face, the feeling in his green-gray eyes made her forget everything.

He squeezed her fingers and spoke. 'You know I love you. I did not say it earlier to Amice because I wanted to say it to you first. I loved Cecilia and I will never forget her.'

She felt him tremble after that confession and said quickly, 'That is a good thing, Stephen.' *Please say more. Say about us.*

Perhaps he understood her thought for he swallowed. 'Is it not too soon? You have your son now. I do not want you to feel in any way compelled.' His voice deepened. 'Especially by gratitude.'

She shook her head. 'I will be forever grateful to you, Stephen, for helping me win back Matthew, but — ' She stopped. How could she say this? It had been the growing wish of her heart but until Matthew was with her again all the rest of her life had stuttered and failed. 'I would like more.'

The instant she spoke she felt a flood of despair. *Now I have lost him. Men do not like to be ordered.* Feeling the tell-tale flush in her face she dropped her head.

'Isabella.'

She dared not look at him, even

when she felt his fingers, feather-light, on her cheek and chin.

'Sweet Mistress Angel, how unsure you still are! But that will pass, believe me. You have a man's love now, not a monster's lust.'

She peeped at him and saw him smiling.

'I never thought I would love again, until I saw you.' His knees cracked as he shifted slightly. 'Till I saw you in your golden cage, Mistress Angel, glittering above me. I think I loved you then.'

He kissed her hand and a shimmer of lightning passed over her skin.

'You caught me,' she said softly.

'I did indeed.' Stephen knelt and leaned in to her. 'To catch and to hold?' he asked, half-teasing, half-solemn. 'You and Matthew? He is a sweet boy and a brave little lad, unfussy.'

She basked in his praise, then yelped as her amazing suitor gently tugged her hair.

'Your answer, lady?'

'To marry?'

'Of course.'

She felt she must burst with happiness. 'For my safety?'

His eyes narrowed briefly, then he grinned, looking like a boy again. 'I wondered if you had overheard! And yes, you and your boy will be safer with me. I want you to be safe, Isabella.'

His concern both touched and reminded her. 'Your family, will they be safe at your friend's?'

'For now.' Frowning, Stephen looked north and said, 'Still I confess I will feel easier in my mind when I have got them out of London and sooner rather than later. What of your friend?'

'Amice told me that she let her apprentice know she was on pilgrimage to Canterbury, should anyone come asking.' She watched his face clear and felt relieved herself, although the question still slipped from her lips, 'Are you sure, Stephen?'

'That I love you? How could I not? That I am wild to marry you? How could I not be?'

He kissed her. He had kissed her before but this was a kiss of peace, passion and love all at once. He wrapped his sinewy armorer's arms about her, captured her mouth with his and embraced her in a slow, full way that made her feel naked and back in bed with him.

We are in a monastery, Isabella tried to protest, while somewhere in her floating mind a small thought complained, *I wish he had done it earlier*.

'I watched you sleep all night and having been waiting to do this,' Stephen said, when they finally paused in their kiss. 'Again and again.'

He demonstrated in a way that delighted her, that filled her with a sparkling light and giddiness throughout her body, as if she had drunk down a rainbow. *With Stephen I will gladly submit to the act of love.*

Perhaps I may even like it. Look how we are with kisses, already intoxicated with each other. Surely more still will be even better?

She could only hope.

8

Stephen plighted his troth to Isabella with Amice and the Abbot of the monastery as witnesses. Matthew chuckled through the brief ceremony and afterwards ran to Stephen to be plucked off his feet and flung into the air. Stephen obliged the little lad and then turned to his betrothed.

'We should leave.'

They set out soon after, making for the house of Stephen's friend Thomas Smith.

★ ★ ★

'Daddy!'

Joanna flung herself at Stephen. She was red-faced, but not, he realized quickly, because she was whooping or finding breathing difficult. She pressed her hot little arms around his neck, all but choking him.

'Daddy!'

Careless of tools, ashes or anything else in Tom's workshop he sat down with her on the anvil and hugged her tight. Tears threatened to storm into his eyes and he fought them back.

'My thanks.' He held out an arm to Thomas and the two men shook hands, then Stephen returned his attention to Joanna, blowing a noisy raspberry on her throat, which delighted his girl.

'Will you introduce us, brother?' Bedelia's crisp question bit into his reunion.

Blinking at the reminder, Stephen saw Amice, looking Thomas up and down in an appreciative manner and Isabella hovering on the threshold, clasping Matthew by the hand. Sympathy swept through him in a warm tide as he spotted the crease of worry on his newly-betrothed's forehead. *To Isabella, families are a threat.*

He blew a second raspberry on Joanna's neck and pointed. 'Here is a lady I have been hoping you and your aunt would meet.'

Joanna looked across the workshop and leaned against her father to say, in a loud whisper, 'She is all golden, like an angel.'

'I think so too.'

'Will she help my breathing?'

'I believe she will,' answered Stephen steadily, though his heart bled for his child. 'Has that troubled you?'

'Not so much.' Joanna shrugged and stared at Isabella again. 'Will she give me a lock of her golden hair as a breath charm?'

Across the room Isabella gave a small, decisive nod.

'I am sure of it. Her name is Isabella and there is Matthew, her boy, and Amice, her friend.'

Alerted to the others, Joanna grinned at Matthew and studied Amice closely before sliding from her father's knee. She walked across to the spice seller, her wide brown eyes never leaving the tall, dark-skinned, beautiful woman.

'Will you be my friend, too?'

Amice crouched and ruffled the child's hair. 'Yours and Matthew's.' Producing a small bag of marbles from her gown, she knelt on the beaten earth floor. In moments, Matthew and Joanna had joined her. She looked over their intent heads and winked at Stephen. 'Now you can talk.'

* * *

She had been welcomed. Braced for questions and censure, Isabella busied herself pouring wine and passed the cups around the others seated at the trestle table in the corner of the workshop. She started as Stephen brushed her hand.

'You do not need to work to justify your place,' he said softly.

She nodded, convinced yet not entirely comfortable. Still she felt the good humor of Thomas, big and bluff, and even Bedelia, busy and shrewd. It was lovely to be accepted, yet unfamiliar.

'My turn!'

Off in another corner, Matthew flicked a marble and Joanna cheered it on. The two youngsters tussled with Amice as if they had been playmates for years, warring like puppies. *They even have a look of each other, around the nose and chin, and could be brother and sister.*

She glanced at Stephen and he smiled at her, his eyes crinkling in the corners in the way that she loved. He raised his cup to her and she almost jumped up to fetch the wine jug again, but then recalled what he had said.

He leaned right across the trestle and kissed her. 'Easy, angel,' he murmured, closing his eyes to a ribald comment from one of the apprentices polishing helmets and shields at the back of the workshop.

'If my brother will sit down again, perhaps we can return to business?' Bedelia instantly undermined her crisp comment by exchanging a conspiratorial glance with Isabella. 'You see how he is, Isabella? I think all armorers are the same. They never do today what they can put off until tomorrow.'

'Your sister slanders us.' The bearded, balding Thomas crossed his fingers over his big belly, 'but we are large enough to take it.'

This is how a family can be, Isabella thought. *I never realized.*

'I — No, I cannot wait any more.' Stephen slapped his palm on the table. 'I must say this now. Joanna, Matthew, are you listening? My mistress Isabella has agreed to become my wife. We are betrothed.'

'Excellent,' said Bedelia, after a small, satisfied silence, tapping her fingers against her cup. 'I look forward to seeing a splendid ring for her, Stevie.'

Isabella breathed again.

'Now you will be my mother, too.' Joanna put her thumb in her mouth and sucked contentedly. 'You here and Mama Cecilia in heaven.'

'Stevie,' Matthew repeated, as he flicked another marble.

'I have spices to scent your bridal gown,' said Amice, waggling her dark eyebrows in a way that made Isabella blush.

She felt herself blushing harder when Stephen strode round the trestle and planted a full kiss on her mouth. 'See, my sweet?' he said, kissing her again as the whole workshop burst into wild applause. 'You are already beloved.'

* * *

After that, Isabella expected that no one would want to be serious or sit to discuss how to defeat the Martinton clan once and for all. Again this family and their friends surprised her. Once everyone had kissed and hugged each other, Stephen strolled to the open doorway, looked out into the alley and then closed the door.

When he turned back, he looked older, grimmer. 'I have a place in Kent, an old holding of my family's. Tomorrow, we shall go there. It will be safer and out of reach of spies.'

'Agreed,' said Thomas, reaching down from his bench seat to fondle a gray cat that had slipped in through the closing door.

'Leave the city?' Isabella had not anticipated that. 'Flee London?'

Stephen chuckled at her expression and shook his head. 'The country may not have the streets and wharfs and people, my sweet, but it does not have the stink or trouble, either.' He nodded to the children, their heads bent over their play as Amice helped Joanna and Matthew create the form of a mermaid on the floor from scraps of metal, straw and rags. 'A healthy place for little ones.'

'But Isabella is right.' Amice looked up from her outline of the mermaid and fixed Stephen with a dark, compelling glance. 'What is the point of burying yourself in the country when the goldsmiths will be always after you? For make no mistake. Stephen, the guild may not like the Martintons but they will support them. Sir William will argue that a certain person' — Amice nodded to Matthew — 'is Richard Martinton's heir.'

Rage burst through Isabella. 'They would and yet look how they treated him! Underfed, ignored, neglected.' She wanted to storm across the workshop and sweep her child up, but Stephen stepped across her path. 'I am all right,' she snapped, as his arms enfolded her.

'I know you are,' he replied, controlled as only a smith used to working with molten metals could be, adding, for her ears only, 'You do not smother those you love.'

Though she knew it was unworthy, his very ease made her want to fight, the more so when Stephen said, 'Amice is right. We need to be free of them for good.' He glanced at Matthew, doodling contentedly on the floor. 'Inheritance?'

She shuddered at the idea. Yes, her boy should have his rights, but she could not stand the thought of dealing with Sir William. 'Not if it puts me or mine in their power again.'

'That makes it easier,' Stephen went on calmly. Releasing her, he escorted her back to the bench and waited until she had sat down again before he settled beside her. 'It will be far less troublesome if I do not have to be too concerned with his rights there.'

'But, brother, will the child not resent it when he is older?' Bedelia dropped in.

Stephen leaned down and stroked the gray cat himself. 'He will do very well as my boy,' he asserted, dismissing the whole inheritance matter in a splendid, almost regal manner. *Yes, he understands that this giving up of rights is almost unheard of, but appreciates that I cannot stand to have any more dealings with the Martintons. I want Matthew free of them and safe.* Isabella clenched her fists under the table. What Stephen said made perfect sense and yet, contrary-wise, part of her was suddenly angry again. *I wish it was not so unfair. My boy does not deserve such losses. We have both suffered for nothing.* Did Stephen understand that, too, or was he too logical?

Stephen twisted about on the bench to face her. 'These goldsmiths are powerful men but even though they may consider me a blacksmith I have influence. Do you know of anything that we can use against them?'

There was a warrior under that coolness, Isabella realized, as she glared up into his stone face. Strangely, his anger and indignation comforted her. Even as she replied, 'Nothing! They told me nothing!' she began to remember.

'Yes?' prompted Stephen and Bedelia together. Amice and Thomas grinned at their joint question.

'A seal or seals?' Trying to recall exactly what had been said, or rather not said, Isabella pressed her fingers against her forehead. Seals were commonplace things, used by people on their letters and documents. A wax seal attached to a letter was an added proof of the sender's identity. 'No, I am sorry. That is all I have. My mother-in-law spoke of them once and Sir William instantly stopped her. I remembered that as strange but it probably means nothing.'

Next instant she gasped as Stephen snatched her even closer and tickled her, exactly as she tickled Matthew. 'All you have? All you have? With this we can defeat them!'

'Sto . . . p!' Isabella giggled, but he kept on tickling and then Joanna and Matthew piled in with crooked fingers and noisy calls. All thoughts of revenge and even what Stephen meant was lost amidst laughter and horse-play.

★ ★ ★

After supper, Stephen was determined to have Isabella to himself for a time, whatever their final sleeping arrangements. He suggested she join him at the stables, 'to look over a pony for Matthew.'

141

Isabella agreed with such haste that he felt ashamed, the more so when she sped to the barn as if expecting to see a docile little beast already saddled for her son. Stepping after her into the high-roofed building, Stephen saw her shaking her head.

'I did not think there would be any ponies.'

'No, I am sorry, but — ' Spotting the teasing sparkle in her eye, he stopped and laughed. 'You knew!'

'But I still came.' She wagged a finger, smiling when he caught it. 'You do realize it will be Matt who asks you from now until Christmas time about his horse? Children have prodigious memories when it comes to expected presents.'

Feeling very amiable he enfolded her again in his arms. 'He can have one for Christmas and Kentish country to ride in.'

'And Joanna, too. Have you a knife about you for me to cut a lock of hair for her?'

Pleased she was thinking of his daughter, he said, 'Joanna already has a pony, and I shall trim your hair.' *I must give her a good knife. And take a lock of that wondrous hair for myself, too. Who knows? Maybe Joanna is right and it will be a luck charm.*

'That is well.' She walked her fingers up his chest. 'As far as a horse is concerned, perhaps you could give Matthew Ulysses.'

He laughed aloud at the idea of the tiny boy on his old gray, delighted to find her so playful. Isabella had endured much, but she was young and now she had her son.

'Stevie . . . '

Hearing his sister's nickname hesitantly on Isabella's lips he pointed to the hay-loft. 'Shall we go up?'

She went ahead of him up the wooden ladder, nimble and quick. Following after he was not altogether surprised when she pushed him into a mound of sweet-smelling hay and sprawled on top of him.

'Now you have me, madam, what next?' he teased.

She stared back at him, desire and uncertainty both bright in her face.

'You do not have to do anything,' he said softly.

She rolled away, fell to biting her fingernails. 'I want to, but this is not my way of saying thanks, I can never thank you enough,' she confessed rapidly.

'We love each other. In love there are no games of gratitude or debts.'

'I feel the same.' She gnawed at her lower lip, then burst out, 'Why am I suddenly so angry at times?'

Stephen cocked his head on one side. 'With me?'

Her eyes darkened. 'Even with you.' She clenched her fists. 'You are so reasonable.'

He shrugged, keeping matters light although he knew these were things of shade. 'For years you have not been able to be angry. Now you can indulge.'

She frowned, looking ready to protest, but he went on, seeking to show her that he understood. 'And all alloys take time to meld.'

'Alloys?'

'Is that not what marriage is?'

Her face fell. 'I do not know.'

She is eighteen and has known no men but brutes. 'Let me teach you, Mistress Angel.'

She glanced at him, a wicked tease that gave him heart and pleasure together. 'A seven year apprenticeship?'

He chuckled and kissed the tip of her nose. As she scowled he eased his arms about her, then plucked a strand from the hay and put it in his mouth, to make her laugh. When she found a feathery grass top and tickled his face with it he reckoned they were making progress.

I shall court her. We shall court each other. It will not take seven years, perhaps not even seven days. She is a passionate creature who needs a little space to heal, a little time to know she can trust me. I shall ask Tom if we can stay on, just for a few more days.

A few more days would serve in other ways, too. Duke Henry would be back in London and he had things to tell him.

Isabella does not realize what she saw in that goldsmith's house and workshop, but I do. And it is the means to set her, Matthew and the rest of us free.

9

Isabella was delighted that she and Stephen stayed in the hay barn for so long, until long past nightfall and moon-rise. They lay side by side in their soft, scented bower and talked. He told her of his childhood in Kent and the delights that awaited her and Matthew. He told her of serving as an apprentice. She told him of London, and its gossipy, quarrelsome warm-hearted folk, of the alleyways close to *The Street*, of how she had met Amice.

She did not speak of her marriage to Richard. She knew Stephen understood her silence and that she did not need to tell him, unless she chose. That freedom was a wonder to her and, she guessed, another gift of love. *He loves me. That is the true miracle.*

Her Stephen now. *He has helped me rescue my son and we love each other.*

How am I now so lucky?

She knew, too, that he wanted her, but he held off, proving he was no Richard Martinton. That night she slept beside her son in Thomas's workshop, on thick straw pallets. Again, without any long explanation between them, Stephen understood her need to be close to Matthew. 'It lets him know you are there with him in the night,' he said, tactfully turning the matter about.

'It will not be for long,' Isabella said quickly.

His slow smile steadied her. 'I know.'

During the next day and the days that followed, Stephen was attentive and affectionate, giving her light kisses and tiny caresses. After supper and evenings was their special time, out in the hay-barn. To Isabella's mingled delight and embarrassment, everyone knew it. By the second evening Joanna and Matthew were even opening the workshop door and pointing the way for them, giggling in joint and happy unity.

'I thought we were hurrying to Kent?' she asked, on their third evening together.

Stephen shook his head. 'No need for haste now,' he answered mysteriously.

'Then your work?' she persisted.

He stroked her arm, a sweet tingle. 'My lord is used to my coming and going. And there have been many saints' days of late, times of holiday.'

She had forgotten about the holy days, overwhelmed as she was by concern for her son. 'Amice says that Sir William sent his servant John to her shop yesterday. Her apprentice told the story of her going on pilgrimage and the man went away.'

Stephen nodded. 'They will not find us here. Amice's lad is sensible and he knows how to evade pursuit.'

'But for how long? How long will I have to look over my shoulder to protect my son?' Again the rage was building, hot in her head.

Stephen rolled a little away from her and sat with his feet dangling into the hay loft. 'It will not be for much longer, Isabella, I swear it. When you spoke of seals, I knew we had a weapon against them.'

'How so? Men have seals for letters, yes, but what of it?'

'Because one of the more lucrative, secret and illegal trades in London is in forgery. They are forging seals! Why else was Sir William so alarmed when your mother-in-law mentioned them? Why else the secrecy? Making false seals is an evil crime and, depending on whose seals they are copying, it may be treason.'

Ignoring his large scowl, Isabella settled beside him and dangled her legs over the edge. As fast as it came, her anger burned away, to be replaced by puzzlement. 'Treason?'

'If they are making forgeries of the king's great seal, the one that he attaches to his charters and writs, then that is treason.'

Would the family dare? She thought of Sir William's love of luxury and had

150

her answer. 'We have no proof.'

'It will be found, believe me. Tomorrow, I intend to seek an audience with Duke Henry, who has now returned to his palace at the Savoy. When I tell my lord what I suspect the Martintons are doing, his men will raid their workshops.' Smiling grimly, Stephen stretched his arms above his head. 'Sir William and the rest will never trouble you again, I promise you.'

Never again, a wonderful thought, so large in scope that she could scarcely believe it. In a fierce spurt of joy she almost forgot where she was sitting. Stephen caught her arm and steadied her.

'I think you should come away from that drop,' he growled.

'I will when you do. Matthew and I will be free to walk in London before we go on to your manor house in Kent?' she added quickly, to divert him.

'If it pleases you.' Stephen trailed a fingertip over her left breast. 'Though 'manor house' sounds very grand. It is simply a home.'

'A home for all of us.' It was so lovely to be able to say that.

'Yes, it is that.' He rubbed noses with her. 'Are you eager to be out and about in your city again?' he asked.

She nodded.

'Would you like to stroll out now, Mistress Angel? The evening is fine.'

Startled, Isabella glanced back at the inviting piles of hay and tried to quell her disappointment and yes, her resentment. 'If you like.' She wondered if she sounded sulky.

Keeping her face composed, she watched Stephen swing his legs round and step away from the drop. Copying him, she did not think she had revealed any of her feelings but gasped now as he suddenly snared her in a fierce embrace.

'This is what I like,' he told her, kissing her lips and hands and throat. 'I think you do, too, or should I stop?'

'No,' she said quickly, turning so he could cup her breasts. 'Do not stop,

Stephen, please.'

He lifted her in his arms and laid her down in the hay. He enfolded and caressed and undressed her, saying how very beautiful she was. He told her he loved her, over and over. He coaxed her to undress him and when she called him beautiful, he laughed.

Slowly and very sweetly, they joined. For her, and for the first time in her life, she understood how man and woman could truly be one. Fearing pain and tearing, she knew only dizzying, glorious pleasure, followed by a hot, sweaty, salty tenderness.

And then more, again, much more . . .

$\star$ $\star$ $\star$

That night she and Stephen slept in the hay loft — when they slept at all.

10

'I must come with you. Yes, Duke Henry has summoned you, Ste, but this concerns me and mine.'

'Ste' was Isabella's new nickname for him. Stephen was not sure if he liked it and he certainly disapproved of her idea of flitting with him to the Savoy. He drummed his fingers on his belt and looked down his nose at her. A few days ago, his maddening little wench would have argued or paled when he glowered. Now she merely tapped her foot. A pretty foot, clad in a new boot, but then she was pretty altogether and regaining weight.

'And Matthew?' *Surely mentioning her son will stop this mad idea.*

Isabella took a deep breath, as if to blow away the eddying breeze that plucked at her skirts and hair. 'Amice and Thomas are walking back to her shop today. Matthew and Joanna are desperate to go with them. Please, Stephen, the children are going wild, cooped up like doves in a cote. Let them go out with them. And let me come with you.'

She was hard to resist when she pleaded, but he tried. 'What if this whole matter goes against me?'

The instant he spoke he knew he had made a mistake. Isabella pounced on it at once. 'Then you must not go, either.'

He snorted. 'One does not ignore a duke.'

'As your betrothed I should be with you, to support you, Ste.'

No, I do not like Ste as a pet name, but that will keep. This could be life and death. 'There may be a trial by ordeal.' He planned to wear chain mail and take his weapons, ready to fight.

Isabella straightened and tilted up her chin, trying to make herself look taller. The rising wind howled behind her as she declared, 'I should be the one to undergo it. I heard of the seals. I told you of them. If your duke requires witnesses then he will need to question me.'

'No, I want you safe.' He rubbed the tight muscles at the back of his neck, wishing the weather would whip into a roaring gale, to keep her at home. 'Sir William and his kin may be there.'

'I would like to face them. I would like to win over them, just once.'

A score for her and a natural desire but, staring at his determined, breeze-blown angel, Stephen felt an ashy despair. 'I could not bear the thought of you or Matt at risk, Isabella. It would hamper me.'

Now she did pale. 'I had not considered that. I am sorry.' She looked away from him to the pink dawn seeping round the roof-tops and scratched at her hand, a trick she did when nervous.

'Why can Isabella not go with you?' His sister stepped into the courtyard and closed on them rapidly. 'Has she not spent enough time waiting on others?'

Isabella blushed a deep rose but Bedelia was far from finished. 'Those wretched Martintons are not God. Duke Henry has more sense than to give them victory. Take her with you to the Savoy, Stevie. You will both be easier.'

Stephen knew he was beaten. He threw up his hands, biting back the question, 'Did you put her up to this?' to his anxious betrothed. Isabella did not do those kind of underhand things. *And how would you like to be left behind? Not much.* 'Very well! Can you walk in those new boots?'

'Yes, Stephen,' said Isabella quickly.

She looked so meek and biddable he wanted to take her to bed again, although they had only just risen from the hay loft. Contenting himself with kissing her, Stephen opened the gate through which they could walk down to the Thames to pick up a wherry. 'Come then, before I change my mind.'

★   ★   ★

For the third time that month Isabella found herself at the enormous palace of the Savoy as she and Stephen were escorted by three liveried servants of Lord Henry toward the ducal apartments set behind the great hall. *One day I might come here and be at ease and happy, but not today.* The palace was vast, its grounds sprawling, its servants endless, but what were these things to her? As she and Stephen crossed a courtyard the sneaking breeze snapped at her ankles and nipped her ears, reminding her, though she needed no reminders, of others who had pinched and bullied her.

I may meet Richard's family here. I must be prepared. She cast her mind back to what Sir William and her mother-in-law had said about seals but could think of nothing new. She felt a squeeze on her hand.

'Not far and not long now.' Stephen, his dark hair twirled by the breeze, gave her a comforting smile. 'Whatever happens, you and Matthew will remain together. Duke Henry swore as much to me.'

A glint in his eyes made her gasp. 'You compelled the duke to swear this?' she said softly, conscious, though Stephen seemed unconcerned, of those liveried servants.

'I suggested that if he wanted me to testify he should do so.' He laughed at her expression and swung her hand. 'Be not so worried, Mistress Angel. My lord is a fair man.' He tugged her closer and dropped a kiss on her trembling mouth. 'And he will adore you.'

His green-gray eyes twinkled at her, reminding her of a form of lapis lazuli. And there was something about that brilliant, blue-green stone that was important, that Sir William had said, or done, some action.

She creased her forehead and scratched her fingers, striving to remember. Beside her Stephen dipped his head as they entered a cloistered walk, then sneaked a kiss from her as the shadows briefly hid them.

'Stephen!'

He grinned. 'Better than Ste, at least.'

So she would have to find another pet name. And he had done it. He had diverted her and now as she relaxed a little the vital memory shimmered through and she caught it.

'What?' he said.

She shook her head. She could be mysterious.

They turned round one corner of the cloister — straight into three more servants of the duke, bringing Sir William and his party. There were over a dozen of them, Isabella realized with a sickening jolt, and every man armed to the teeth. Her nerves already at screaming pitch, she heard the screech of a blade and saw sparks on the cloister wall as a squire in Sir William's party clumsily drew his sword.

'Traitor!' roared Sir William, spitting the word as his whole party charged, ignoring and even cutting at the duke's people in their rush to reach her.

It was madness and Isabella felt it

herself. As Stephen leapt forward to shield her, she jumped sideways, screaming, 'Here, then, here!' and drew her dagger — the sharp, honed dagger that Stephen had given her.

With yells, bared weapons and whirling arms the gaudy column surged like a sea breaker toward her, but Stephen lunged and shielded her again, his sword arm faster than lightning. One of Sir William's men screamed and toppled, clutching a gaping, pumping wound in his chest. Another slipped on the blood and crashed against a pillar, crumpling into a dark, twitching heap. Stephen charged a second time and another man screamed, his cry cutting off abruptly as he fell. Backing up against another pillar, Isabella saw a blur of movement from the corner of her eye as a man tried to come at Stephen from his blind side.

'No!' She slashed with her puny knife, ducking as a blade sparked down the pillar toward her. She could not escape its lethal track . . .

A huge hand clamped round her arm and yanked her away. Stephen whirled and dropped her behind him, roared and took guard again, the cloister echoing with his battle cry.

'Stand fast! Hold!' called another voice, clear and cold. More armed men spilled along the cloister walk, swiftly and efficiently disarming Sir William and his people. Stephen lowered his sword and closed his eyes.

'You have convinced me, Stephen.' Pale, lean and elegant, Duke Henry stalked into his own cloister and took in the scene. 'Now I will hear the rest. Within the treasure room, I think.'

Why there, Isabella wondered, before she recollected that Stephen had mentioned that the French King was a hostage within this palace. *The duke will not want the king of the French to hear unsavory tales of forged great seals and the London goldsmiths.* Her chest tightened at what was to come. *However this story of seals spins out, please let the duke believe us.* Fast on the heels of that reflection came another; more a clammy feeling of rising panic and a heart-felt plea than a thought. *Please, please, let Stephen be safe, Stephen and my son.*

Reaction was setting in, from the shock of the fight. Already it seemed a distant event, half a legend. *Stephen and I were attacked at the Savoy by the kindred of my dead husband.* She shuddered and her jaw would not work as she tried to mouth thanks to her betrothed.

Time felt to have slowed down, but now she realized only an instant had passed. The duke walked up, his dark eyes very kind. To her amazement, he offered her his arm. 'My lady.'

'No lady,' hissed Margery Martinson from somewhere behind Sir William. 'The morals of a mermaid. She will not keep her latest paramour for long — '

'I will have silence,' the duke said, and now there was.

★ ★ ★

Within the treasure room, Stephen lost no time in standing beside Isabella, a public show of support. *I am her betrothed and husband-to-be. Hurt her and you must deal with me.* Besides, she was so wan he feared she might faint, especially as she swayed slightly on her feet. He looked at his lord, a silent plea that Isabella be given a chair. She kept glancing at him now, her blue eyes wary and shuttered, as if she expected him to tear her head off for leaping to defend him.

I am not so unfair, though I admit you startled me. He had surely lost a year of his life in worry when she had pitched herself into the fray. *Her own family by marriage, attacking her! What bastards.* Striving to keep his temper, he tapped his sword belt. It was a great relief that the duke clearly liked her, but even though he trusted his lord, a worm of disquiet still squirmed within his head. *The sooner I get you down to the country, my sweet, the better.*

It amused and rather gratified him

that she could stand amidst this mort of
treasure and still be staring at him, a
slow up and down look as if she was
checking he was truly unhurt. She
flicked a sideways glance at the
dark-robed duke, seated on his chair on
a small dais at the back of the room,
but she spared no looks for Sir William
and his allies, nor any for the heaps of
treasure ranged round them.

It was hot and stuffy in the packed,
windowless chamber, with men and a
few women arranged in a semi-circle
about the dais, but no one was in
danger of dozing.

Attentive as a hound on point, Duke
Henry leaned forward. 'A seat for my
lady Isabella.'

At once a stool was found and
brought. Stephen breathed out a long
sigh of relief as Isabella sank onto the
seat. The duke smiled at her, candle-
light glinting on his fair hair. 'Will you
have a glass of malmsey, my lady? I
believe you know wine and I trust you
will like this.'

Without waiting for an answer, Duke Henry snapped his fingers and only Stephen understood that his lord's small frown was due to gout, which plagued him. Everyone else stared at the floor tiles while the message went out through the palace corridors.

Moments later, as he watched a server push through the lines of people to pour the duke and Isabella glasses of wine, Stephen reflected on what Duke Henry had said. *So my lord has looked into her background. Is that good?* He could only hope it was.

'The wine is fine, my lady?' the duke asked, as Isabella took a sip.

'It is excellent, my lord.' Hearing her gentle, clear answer, Stephen was relieved afresh, less so when his lord nodded and said, 'To business, then.'

'We should wait for Sir Nicholas,' said Sir William at once, gathering allies, Stephen guessed. But the duke shook his head.

'You have sufficient with your kindred, Sir William,' he said mildly, adding with more bite, 'I do not feel my palace will withstand any more numbers of your goldsmith's guild.'

'But, my lord, Sir Nicholas is — '

'Late,' said Duke Henry. 'We begin now.'

Here we go. Checking his weapons were still good in case he should be challenged, Stephen braced himself, ready to give an account and sink Sir William and his kin forever.

★   ★   ★

The arguments raged and Isabella listened closely, horribly aware that the fate of her son and her own future happiness were at stake. Stephen spoke first, of seals and forgery, of Sir William and his kin so fearful of discovery of their illegal enterprise that they attacked him and her before the duke could hear their account.

'Yet my men have found no sign of any fake seals at the workshops of Sir William,' remarked the duke.

'Because there are none,' Sir William interrupted, and now he launched into a lengthy counter-argument, fixing on her. According to her uncle by marriage she was a liar, an unfit mother and a wanton. 'She has seduced your poor armorer by her wiles and by wicked magic,' Sir William finished gravely.

'All lies.' Stephen threw his glove on the floor tiles between himself and the portly goldsmith. 'I challenge you or any of your champions.'

'N — ' Isabella bit down on her protest. To honor Stephen's love she should support him. Through burning eyes she watched the duke seated across from her smooth his clean-shaven narrow chin.

'There has been enough fighting for one day.' Duke Henry looked directly at her. 'What do you say in reply to these accusations, my lady? Are you a witch? You certainly appear to have charmed my armorer.'

Isabella looked at Stephen. He would not meet her eye. For an instant she doubted. *Does he think I have bewitched him?* Then she thought of all their time together, their joy in each other and their children, and her world steadied again.

With a graceful acknowledgment to the duke, Isabella rose, but before she could answer him, her mother-in-law shoved through the mass of people. Clearly seeing her chance, the older woman fought her way to the gap at the front of the room to address Duke Henry.

'You will hear her, my lord, before me, a good Christian woman who lost her son to this creature?' Encouraged by the stunned silence, Margery went on. 'My boy married her to put an end to a dispute between two families. She could not even bring that peace.'

'Why was that?' the duke inquired.

Margery did not want to answer that. She puffed up her chest like a strutting hen. 'Her care of my grandson is negligent. As for her latest paramour, a man no better than a smith — '

The burning fuse that had been lit in Isabella's head by these grotesque accusations exploded. 'My care of Matthew?' she interrupted, stepping forward to face the buxom matron. 'My little boy, whom you tore from me and kept from me for months? My son whom your kinsman threatened with violence? Matthew was underfed and neglected when Stephen and I tracked him to Kent! As for my lord being a smith, I am proud of that. I am proud of him.'

'Wait.' Stephen stopped her. 'They threatened a four year old? You did not tell me.'

I dared not, beloved, can you not understand that? I feared exactly your reaction. Wordlessly she tried to express that thought but Stephen scowled and she hated his displeasure. 'I am sorry, Stephen, but . . . But Sir William said that unless I did as he asked he would beat Matthew.'

Before any could react, even the duke's men, Stephen wordlessly drew his sword and ran at the goldsmith.

'Stephen!' Isabella snatched at his arm, trying to hold him, but it was like trying to stop a swinging hammer. He tore through her flailing grip and stormed on.

'Fletcher!' roared the duke. 'Stand down!'

There was a mighty clash of swords. John, Sir William's servant, desperately defended his master as Stephen used his own blade like a deadly scythe.

'I have proof!' Isabella yelled, above the shouts of the rest. She flew from the stool onto the dais and dropped to her knees beside the duke. 'The fake seals are hidden in a jewel box with a false lid inlaid with green lapis lazuli. Please, my lord, set your men to search for that box.'

'Go,' said the duke, nodding to a group of men guarding the door. His voice and expression were mild but his eyes were sharp. 'You recall that very late, my lady.'

'I know.' Terrified the duke might consider Stephen part of this treason,

Isabella gabbled, 'I saw but did not understand, my lord. Not until today, this very day. My master Stephen knew no part of it, I swear.'

Duke Henry caught her hands and turned them, noting the old scratch scars. He studied her face and Isabella endured his keen gaze flicking to the scar on her forehead where Richard had hit her, the scar on her left ear where Richard had belted her. Whatever he saw must have been enough, for he nodded. 'Very well.' He released her. 'You go to Stephen now.'

Skidding across the floor tiles in her haste, Isabella saw John disarmed by a looming Stephen. As his servant crawled away, Sir William's ruddy face turned sickly gray. He slumped down, lifting his hands to shield himself. Margery was already shrieking.

'Stephen,' Isabella said urgently. 'He is not worth it. Please.'

As if he was a man of metal, Stephen turned slowly to her. His eyes were as cold as she had ever seen them.

'I will gladly take him,' said the duke, behind them both. 'In justice he is yours, Fletcher, but even so. I will defer to a lady.'

'Please,' she said again. 'For yours and mine.'

'For you, beloved, and no other,' Stephen growled, but he allowed his sword to clatter to the floor. The next moment she had him safe in her arms — or was she in his? It did not matter.

The duke rose. 'Take him, Lady Isabella. You are truly worthy of each other and clearly deep in love with no magic but caring. I shall make you a grant of land and expect to dance at your wedding. Now go. Leave your erstwhile . . . *relations* to me.'

'My son, my lord,' Isabella began, determined to have that matter also put beyond doubt. Even as she sought to frame the question, the duke anticipated her.

'Matthew — that is his name, yes? Matthew will be forever in your care and your new lord's. You may be certain he shall lose no portion of his rights. I intend to have words with Sir Nicholas on that issue, very soon.'

Heart hammering, Isabella dropped a curtsey. This was more, far more, than she had hoped. She glanced at Stephen, who still glowered at the goldsmiths. She was not certain he had even heard. 'My lord?'

'Go,' the duke interrupted her. 'Take him away. Feed him, sit with him, love him and your son. Go on.'

As the duke's men escorted them out, Isabella could hear Sir William's desperate pleading. Sir Nicholas and the other foremost members of the goldsmith's guild were yet to appear — clearly a prudent choice on their part.

'Do not feel sorry for him,' Stephen warned, speaking for the first time in an age as he received his sword back from one of the duke's men and sheathed it.

'Sorry?' She was astonished he should think that. 'My uncle lost all

174

kinship to me when he threatened to hurt my son!'

'Agreed. And now, thanks to the duke, Matthew will have his Martinton rights.'

'You heard that?' *Please be pleased.*

Stephen snorted. 'Sir William made me see blood when he set his miserly brutes on you, but he did not stopper my ears. It is a good result, and just.'

Isabella nodded, sending up a prayer of thanks that Stephen saw it in that way. *Thank the holy mother he is so reasonable.*

They were walking faster now, hurrying to the river. 'How did you remember that hiding place?' Stephen asked her now.

'From your kiss and your eyes,' she said, which was no more than the truth, although Stephen wagged a finger at her, his eyes finally lightening from the storm gray of his earlier dark mood.

'Keep your secret, then, Mistress Angel,' he laughed.

What a relief to see him more himself

again. 'Truly Stephen, I remembered because your eyes are sometimes the same color and I once saw the inlay come away in Sir William's hand. I thought he had broken it but then later saw the jewel box whole again, without repair.'

She stopped a moment as her companion took her cool hand in his warm one. 'I am listening,' he prompted, and chuckled. 'I did not realize you kept such close attention to the color of my eyes, Mistress Angel.'

We are betrothed to be married. I will not blush. I will keep answering. 'It was a box Sir William kept close. I thought it was because he was fond of the decoration, but that moveable inlay meant that the box had a secret compartment.'

'Aye, and a girl in a goldsmith's workshop would notice such things as no repair. Clever lass.' Stephen smiled, weaving his fingers through hers.

'Not so clever. It was only lately that I understood what it meant.' Despite

the warm day she shivered. 'I understood almost too late.' Thinking of it
again, Isabella shook her head. 'Let us
leave this place,' she said, suddenly
weary of intrigue and London. 'Let us
leave tomorrow, for Kent.'

'Gladly, my heart.' Stephen stopped
on the graveled path and kissed her.
'Home it is.'

Epilogue

Duke Henry had indeed danced with her at her wedding. He had sent pink and white gowns and veils for her, Amice, Joanna and Bedelia, and gold and black tunics for Stephen and Matthew. Isabella wore her hair loose and knew she had done the right thing when Stephen ran from the church door to meet her coming to their wedding.

It was a merry ceremony with the apple trees of Kent in blossom, blooming late and just for them, it seemed. Matthew and Joanna held the train of her gown between them and Amice perfumed it with a heady mix of spices that made Isabella long for the evening. There was a dark instant when she considered her parents who, although invited to her wedding had not come, but then her family, her true family, gathered her in and all was well again. When the priest announced them to be man and wife, Stephen kissed her for so long that Thomas joked he could have made a suit of mail in the time.

Finally she and Stephen were alone, within the small barn of his Kent house. Amice talked closely to the duke, perhaps of spices. Everyone else was still drinking and singing inside his thatched cottage. Her son Matthew and her new daughter Joanna were dancing, their little faces bright with glee. Joanna was breathing quickly but well and she looked very pretty in her new gown. She had a new gold necklace round her slender throat, given to her by her father, and she carried a lock of gold hair, given to her by Isabella.

My youngsters are beginning to thrive. And now at last Stephen and I are alone. The barn was theirs, hers and Stephen's. *My husband.*

Isabella laughed when Stephen tossed her over his shoulder and almost ran up the ladder to the loft with her. Set down, she realized that her man had already been busy up here. The loft was adorned with fresh sheets and pillows, sweet hay, sweet flowers, jugs of cowslips and bluebells. He had brought up flagons of wine, ale and cider. There were cups and plates, a basket of pies, cheeses, dates and sugared fruits.

Stephen popped a piece of sugared peel into her mouth. 'Chew, little wife,' he said teasingly.

Chewing, Isabella stared up at him. He looked so splendid in his gold and black tunic, with a gold and black cloak. She swallowed. 'I love you.'

'And I worship you, Mistress Angel, mistress mine.' He swept her up again. 'Let me show you.'

With a rapt, amazed expression, like a man in a dream, he laid her on a soft bed of linen and hay. They made love all that night, with the birds singing them joyously into the next day and Isabella free of shadows and fear, a goldsmith's widow no more, rather a blacksmith's wife.

We do hope that you have enjoyed reading this large print book.

Did you know that all of our titles are available for purchase?

We publish a wide range of high quality large print books including:
Romances, Mysteries, Classics
General Fiction
Non Fiction and Westerns

Special interest titles available in large print are:
The Little Oxford Dictionary
Music Book, Song Book
Hymn Book, Service Book

Also available from us courtesy of Oxford University Press:
Young Readers' Dictionary
(large print edition)
Young Readers' Thesaurus
(large print edition)

For further information or a free brochure, please contact us at:
Ulverscroft Large Print Books Ltd.,
The Green, Bradgate Road, Anstey,
Leicester, LE7 7FU, England.
Tel: (00 44) **0116 236 4325**
Fax: (00 44) **0116 234 0205**

Other titles in the
Linford Romance Library:

MORE THAN A PORTRAIT

Diana Dennison

When Jane is offered a job in northern Italy, with its promise of sunshine and colour, mountains and romantic scenery, her adventurous spirit can hardly refuse. Then she meets her employer: the unpredictable, pompous and dictatorial Duncan Frobisher. Sparks immediately fly between them, and Jane comes to know more than her fair share of elation and black depression before her temporary employment comes to an end . . .

FORGOTTEN

Fay Cunningham

Driving home in the dark, Serena stops to help an injured man lying in a ditch. He mutters something unintelligible, but that is only the start of her problems. Someone is watching the apartment she shares with her brother, her mother is being particularly secretive, and police detective Jack Armstrong is convinced Serena is hiding something. Just when she thinks things can get no worse, her missing father turns up. This is definitely not the time to fall in love.

A PERFECT RHAPSODY

Dawn Bridge

After an unhappy romance with a concert pianist, Emma joins her local orchestra — something she has always wanted to do. Their new young conductor, Paul, seems to be an aloof and arrogant man, but Emma finds herself attracted to him. What secret is he concealing? Will she be able to break through the barrier which he has erected around himself? And how can she ever hope to compete with the beautiful Samantha for his affections, whilst dealing with admirers of her own?

TIDES OF LOVE

Phyllis Mallett

When her widowed father dies, Clarissa Marston is left penniless. George Farand, however, has a solution: in debt to the late Mr. Marston, he invites Clarissa to stay with his family at their Cornish estate of Trevarron until he can repay her the money. She warms to the genial John Farand, despite his darkly brooding brother Edwin. But Trevarron is a place of ominous secrets, and Clarissa begins to fear for her safety — until the handsome Richard Redmond comes to her aid . . .

FATE IN FREEFALL

Ken Preston

Paralysed by grief after losing her fiancé in a skydiving accident, Katrina Maslow cannot allow herself to love another man. She travels the world in an attempt to flee from her former life, ending up in Rio and accepting a job as a guide with J Stone Adventure Trips. But Jay, the handsome owner of the company, is determined to break down her reserves. As they are pursued by a ruthless killer, Katrina finally realises she is in love with Jay — just at the moment she might lose him forever . . .